MW00955822

Blind Date

Ten Short Stories

by

Robert Hobkirk

To Jessica,
Best wishes
Rob Hobkirk
11/15

Also by Robert Hobkirk

Haiku Avenue: 333 haiku poems

Somewhere Poetry Grows Wild Under the Eucalyptus

Copyright

Dedication

This book is dedicated to David, Julie, Kevin, and Keith.

Acknowledgement

Thanks to Jeannine, my loving wife, for putting in the time and work to edit out the typos and glitches. I value her constructive criticism and her genuine interest in my writing.

Table of Contents

Contents

Introduction

These ten stories in *Blind Date* have one thing in common: all the protagonists are struggling. All of creation struggles. A seed, which falls in the shade and sprouts, soon struggles to find a place in the sun. These characters also struggle to find their place in the sun, or, if the day is too hot, a place in the shade. They may not be the best at making wise decisions, but all are righteous, not a rotten apple in the produce aisle.

Blind Date

I was on a blind date of sorts with someone I met on Craigslist. The first instant I saw her, there was something about her that was drawing me to her. Maybe it was her slightly trashy looks. We met at an upscale bar. I figured not meeting at Starbucks was a good idea because the caffeine would make me go on like a babbling, hyper idiot. She ordered white wine, and I ordered Schweppes tonic water without the booze. The drinks came, and I took a hit.

The first thing she said was, "I don't know how you can drink that stuff straight?"

"You mean without the liquor to kill the taste?"

"Yeah, it's so bitter."

"That's what I like about it. It's bitter like me. We match."

"You mean you're a grumpy old man?"

"Right. Can't help it. That's what happens when you get old."

"Well, I'm an optimist."

"I'm an optimist too, just a grumpy optimist."

"Your accent. You don't sound like you've lived long in the City. You like living here?"

"It's okay, but I would rather live in a land of mystics and poets."

"What would that be like, and where would you find such a place?"

"What would it be like to live in a land of mystics and poets? And where would I look for such a place? I think it exists only in my imagination."

She asked, "Would you recognize a real poet, the genuine article, not some knockoff?"

"For sure. He would carry his poetry in a plastic bag."

She grimaced. "A plastic bag? What kind of plastic bag?"

"Like a Kohl's bag, or Target."

"I think I get it. No pretentions. No Gucci." She lifted the corner of her expensive bag. "And why mystics?"

"Because they see the humor in the situation. The irony. The great big, pregnant pause in the universe before every calamity."

"Wasn't there a laughing Buddha?"

"You mean the fat little guy with the pot belly sitting on top of the TV?"

"Yeah, that's the one."

"I don't know that much about Buddha, other than he died of food poisoning." I took a swig of tonic water, and its bitterness tightened up my thinking, bringing me back to earth, back from the land of haze.

"You sure about that?"

"Not really. Like I said, I don't know that much about Buddha. But I know that Thomas Merton killed himself by stepping out of the shower, into a puddle where an electric fan was running. Zap! And he was a big fan of the Buddha."

"There's a moral to the story, I'm sure."

"It's good to know the secrets of the universe but better to have common sense and practical knowledge. Like don't step in puddles with electric fans."

"Make sure to close the shower door."

"Exactly."

"And you've got practical knowledge?"

"I have trouble changing a light bulb."

"Too bad. I always wanted a man who could fix things around the house."

"I always wanted a woman who could cook. How about you? Can you cook?"

"Not very well."

"There you go. It all balances out."

"You think it was an accident?"

"No, I think it's because you aren't interested in cooking."

"I mean about Merton."

"Could have been the CIA or more likely the Vatican."

"Blaming the CIA is such a cliché."

I thought, "Oh, oh. I've alienated her by calling her pretentious because of her bag and that she can't cook because she doesn't care. I'm sure she's sick of me being so friggin witty. It's almost time for her to check her phone and say she has to go."

"You're right. It is a cliché," I agreed with her.

"Relax. You aren't a jerk, at least not a big jerk. I've kissed a few princes and found only toads. Tell me some more about Merton. Loved the title of his book Seven Story Mountain. Ever read it?"

"No, never did. But I met a monk once who knew Merton. They were monks together in Kentucky."

"What did he have to say about him?"

"All he could do was bad-mouth Merton. The old Monk said, 'He called himself a monk, but he wasn't a monk. Him with his private hut and all, huh.'"

"Really?"

"Yeah, really. It was a real eye opener. Real disillusionment. Not about Merton, but about being a monk. I went to this Trappist monastery in Northern California, just on a retreat. I wanted to check it out. Thought about becoming a monk and finding enlightenment. Saw this old monk who seemed to glow. Thought I could learn something from him. Then he hits me with bad-mouthing Merton. The old monk said he had been a monk for over fifty years. This is what you get after fifty years, a sour disposition about someone who has been dead for over thirty. I can get just as sour on my own without all the Hail Marys, thank you very much."

"How many monks at this place?"

"About thirty, I guess."

"At least they're trying. Trying to find some happiness."

"I was trying for more than happiness. Going for the cosmic high, something that can only be found by finding God. Heaven on earth. Decided I wouldn't find it at the monastery, not after talking to the old monk."

"You still looking for heaven on earth?"

"Nah, I'm happy being depressed."

"You're funny," she laughed.

"One fat, dumb and happy Buddha, laughing until the TV blacks out, that's me."

We talked for a couple hours or more that seemed like only fifteen minutes. She laughed at all my jokes, and never once did she complain about her parents. I think I was starting to fall in love. I wanted to see her again.

Finally she said, "What time is it?"

"Almost eleven."

"Eek! Didn't realize it was that late. I've got to go."

"Sure. I enjoyed this evening." Now it was over. I wondered how she would brush me off. "Can I help you get a cab?"

"Yeah, you can do that."

She got up. I helped her on with her coat. She got her white cane, tapping it ahead of us as I walked with her outside, holding her arm. A yellow taxi pulled up, and I opened the door for her. She abruptly grabbed me by my jacket and kissed me on my plastic mask. She placed her free hand on the cheek of my mask. "What's that?" she asked, a little shocked.

"I guess I should have told you. That's a cosmetic mask I have to wear when I'm out in public. I had an accident, horrible burns on my face. It scares people when they see it."

"So you wanted to meet me because I'm blind?" she didn't seem angry but a little put off.

"Guilty."

"Don't say guilty. You did nothing wrong, just looking for a little happiness. What's so wrong about that? Like you said, it balances out. Meet me here tomorrow night, same time."

A Perfect Life

I was about ten, helping my mother make up a bed with clean sheets. She was always working.

"Mom," I said, "the neighbor has kittens. Can we get one?"

"You want one?"

"Yeah, and I'll take care of it."

"We'll see."

Mom talked to the neighbor about it. His cat had the kittens under the house and they hadn't come out yet. He told her that if he couldn't find homes for the kittens, they were going to be put in a sack and dumped in the muddy creek. I know this because I was with her when she talked about the kittens. I didn't think he was cold blooded. I just wondered what kind of sack – pillow case or burlap sack. She told him that we would take one when they were a little older and out and about.

The day came when we got our kitten, a cute little calico. For some reason, we didn't give her a name. Maybe we thought that cats didn't get names; they weren't like dogs who always got a name. Cats were creatures living on the borderland of the family and the world. They could easily get along without us, fending for themselves. They didn't need a name to get by. All they needed was not to be put in a sack.

While she was going through the cute kitten stage, she lived in the house. Nothing cuter than a kitten, right? But kittens grow up to be cats real fast. She got to be a certified, gnarly bad ass. No one wanted her on their lap. She could stay outside. Her food and water bowl were put out on the back porch. That was okay with her, the more freedom the better. She could spend her nights ratting, proudly bringing back decapitated, huge grey rats to our back porch in the morning.

"Robbie, get rid of that rat. Throw it in the can," my mom would tell me.

So I would pick up the rat with a piece of newspaper and drop it in the trash can, a fifty gallon drum, in the back yard. It and everything else would get incinerated when we burned our trash once a week. No garbage truck came out where we lived, a neighborhood with dirt roads.

I knew where our cat got the rats, out at the dump.

My mom and dad would take us out to some nice lake from time to time, but parents weren't expected to entertain their kids all the time. We found our own recreation. The dump was our playground, not so much in the summer, but a favorite spot in the winter.

In the winter, the garbage dump didn't look so bad, not like Armageddon, more like a playground. The piles of trash and garbage were covered by snow. The big pit was frozen over where we skated on muddy ice with skates never sharpened. The dirt out of the pit was piled high. We would sled down it and across the ice, our Matterhorn ride with no long line.

In the summer, the dump wasn't so great. Nothing was hidden. It was ugly and not much to do there. One time a bunch of us kids met there for a BB gun fight, playing war. The side I was on had the high ground on top of the hill. The other kids wouldn't come out from their cover and try and take it because they would get shot. Since it turned out rather boring, we never did that again.

There was always a family, a mom and dad and a couple kids, picking up scrap metal and piling it onto the back of their pickup. Someone said they were gypsies, but they looked just like ordinary people to me – no guitars or violins. All the commotion with picking up this and that, caused the rats to get nervous. The rats would scurry here and there, looking for cover. There were plenty of them. They must have been easy pickings for our cat.

Our calico made it through spring and summer, but one fall day we never saw her again. I'm guessing she met with a sudden death at the dump. Ships never sink if they're kept in the harbor. She could kill any rat. Dogs knew not to mess with her. But some people would go there to shoot rats with a .22.

A couple years ago, I went back to the old neighborhood. It had changed, but not for the worse. The dirt road was paved. Our little house that my dad built was still there. The maple sapling had grown into a big tree, covering the whole front yard in cool dark shade. I took the short cut through the woods that we kids used to take to get to the dump. The woods were thick, maybe thicker than back in the day, but the dump wasn't there anymore. It was gone. A community recreation center took its place with picnic tables, a skateboard park, and tennis courts. A swimming pool was just about where the muddy water pit used to be. Families didn't pick through the trash for scrap metal. They paid to have fun.

I'm sure our calico cat was buried somewhere under the manicured sod where once it hunted for rats over piles of trash on Michigan nights lit by moonlight. Her life, sort of living with us, was a perfect life.

Kathy's Struggle

Kathy sat in her dirty, old Chevy, eating two Carl's Jr. breakfast burritos and drinking her 32 ounce Mountain Dew through a straw. A country western station was on the radio with a multimillionaire hillbilly singing about his trials and tribulations with the bottle and the ex-wives. At one minute to seven, she gathered up her unfinished breakfast, her drink, and oversized purse. When she got out of her car, the old Chevy groaned a little, and the left side rose up about three inches. At exactly seven, she was on the doorstep of where she worked, a single story house in the suburbs.

As she was about to ring the doorbell, the door opened. Frowning Mr. Spader stood in the doorway, as if she were a stranger, then stepped aside, motioning her in. He had told her on day one, "Call me Mr. Spader."

Kathy walked into the kitchen, setting her things down on the white tile countertop.

"There was this guy who rear-ended this guy right in front of me on the freeway. I guess God was looking out for me. Could have been me," she said.

"Can't you come a few minutes earlier, just a few minutes earlier," showing his impatience with his tone.

"My shift starts at seven. Right on time," she said, finishing her burrito.

"Yes, but you're eating, and it takes you a few minutes to get organized before you can actually begin work."

"Okay, I'll be ready to go from now on. Is your father awake?" she asked, deflecting the humility of being picked on at seven o'clock in the morning.

"I don't know. I have to get to work. I got some more of that Gold Bond you wanted for his feet. You'll find it on his nightstand. I've got to run, or I'll be late for work."

He got into his white SUV and drove off to his office where he was a manager for the Department of Motor Vehicles in downtown Sacramento on Broadway.

Kathy felt relieved that Mr. Spader had left. He was always complaining about something. Her previous client was off-the-wall abusive, and she got Mr. Spader and his father in their place. She didn't want to complain about another one. Her boss might think that she was just too high maintenance and replace her with someone who wouldn't complain. She was going to stick it out until the old man died. They always did.

She turned on the portable radio she had brought with her. It was already tuned in to the country western station she had been listening to in her car. She thought the music and the "morning zoo" would cheer up Mr. Spader's father, Richard.

She went to the old man's room. He was in his hospital bed, lying on his back, looking up at the ceiling, wondering why he was still alive, wondering what purpose there was in his living.

"Hey, sunshine, how you feeling this morning?" Kathy genuinely felt compassion for the old man.

"Get me up. I have to go."

Kathy got him out of bed and into his wheelchair, took him to the bathroom, and sat him down on the toilet. Her day had begun. Before Mr. Spader got home from work at 5:30, she gave her patient a sponge bath, soothed his itchy skin with ointment, massaged his feet with the Gold Bond, shaved him, helped him brush his teeth, clipped his finger and toenails, changed him out of his pajamas into daytime clothes, changed his bed linen, got him up to eat and watch T.V. and back to bed for rest several times throughout the day, listened to him complain about the President, and talked to him in a friendly, cheerful manner during the day. Richard never said thank you once. For the five months she had been his caregiver, he never said thank you.

During her duties performed this day, she managed to read a 300 page romance novel. She read a novel every day. The reading took her mind off her worries. Her biggest worry was her only daughter, Kim, who was having a hard time finishing high school, but who demanded to go to a private art school costing about $30,000 per year in tuition. Kathy maybe made about $25,000 per year before taxes. But there were school loans, and the school admissions advisor said Kim could automatically get a $10,000 scholarship because she was so talented, which would bring it down to $20,000. And didn't she sell her unicorn drawings at the church bizarre. She had to go to this art school, not the junior college. The teachers had practical experience in the real world – invaluable knowledge. If Kim could just make up a couple classes in summer school, she could get in.

Kathy heard the garage door swing open. Mr. Spader was home. It was time to go home and fix dinner for herself and Kim. Better turn off the radio and stash it in her bag before he started complaining about it. Anything out of the ordinary was a target for complaint. Mr. Spader's teachers didn't have to tell him to color within the lines. She was closing her bag as he walked in the door.

She gave him a nervous greeting. He always made her nervous.

"Everything alright? Everything go okay today?" he asked.

"Oh sure, everything was fine."

"Use the Gold Bond?"

"Sure did. That stuff really works well. I massaged some on his back and also on his feet. Relieves the itch from dry skin."

"Anything else you want to tell me?"

"No, not really. Oh, come to think of it, we need some more disposable bed liners. We're running low."

"I'll get some more tomorrow. You don't mind staying here a little while longer tomorrow while I go to the store, do you?"

"No, I don't mind. See you tomorrow."

"One more thing. Your car looks like it's leaking oil on the street. You should get it fixed. In the meantime if you could just bring some cardboard to put under it, I would appreciate it."

She left, before she started to cry. She got into her car, grabbed the steering wheel, feeling trapped in her powerless state. Her knuckles turned white. She needed something to numb the pain.

On the way home, Kathy stopped off at Wendy's and got her and Kim's supper: a couple cheeseburgers, large chili, large fries, large Coke for each. Kathy didn't smoke, didn't drink, didn't do drugs. Fast food was her addiction. The sugar and salt were like crack. Both she and her daughter had tried all the fad diets to try and lose weight. At first the weight came off, then it came back on. But both she and Kim had low blood pressure. A vegan would be envious of their cholesterol count.

Kathy pulled into her parking space at her apartment complex by the blue dumpster. The smell of a dumpster that hadn't been washed out since it was put in place welcomed her home. She lived in a pink stucco, two story, fifty unit apartment complex built in the 60's. It was built with one idea in mind, maximum profit, which meant getting the most tenants in at the cheapest possible cost. The only thing the owner did for aesthetics was to plant twenty palm trees in one gallon containers back in the day. He thought it was a good idea since the complex was called The Palms. Also, the building code required that something green had to be planted. Over the years, these little palms grew up not to be tall and graceful, but short and stout. They matched the dreams of most of the tenants – stunted. Some were planted too close to each other. The owner thought about thinning them out, but kept putting off the expense.

One day, Oscar was driving by and decided to make the owner an offer for the palms. Oscar was a commercial landscaper, who had a side business that put his kids through college, transplanting palm trees. When he was driving around, out and about, if he spotted a large palm tree, he would approach the property owner about removing the tree. He had the equipment to make what looked like an impossible job quite easy. The housing tracts had plenty of palms that looked just right for the front yard when they were planted, but which grew into towering monsters that looked out of place and a cause of concern by maybe falling over and destroying the house. Sometimes he could get the homeowner to pay him a few hundred to get rid of the thing, but the real money was in reselling it. He sold the palms to large construction projects, like shopping malls and office buildings. He made good money on this little sideline.

He first offered to take the "straggly old palms" out and away for just two thousand, but the owner of The Palms said, "What, you think I'm crazy?" Oscar wound up having to pay two thousand, but he got the ten palms. The owner couldn't refuse a couple thousand in easy money. Oscar would get back his investment on the first tree; after that, it was all profit. The palms were destined to adorn the grounds of a new hospital. Now that the kids had been put through college, the palms were paying for his grandkids' education.

The only thing of visual interest at the apartments, the palms, began to be hauled away while Kathy was at work. She noticed one of the trees was gone. A crater with safety barricades took its place.

Kathy entered her apartment, carrying her bag and the two red and white Wendy paper bags. Kim was on the couch, watching T.V., eating a bag of barbeque potato chips.

"Hey Kim, got us some supper."

Kim didn't bother to greet her mother, just kept munching and staring at the *Judge Judy* show.

Kathy sat a Wendy's bag in Kim's lap and sat down on the couch beside her, setting her food out on a coffee table. Both started in on their cheeseburgers with one hand and their fries with the other.

"There's a big hole out front where there used to be a palm tree. What happened?"

"Don't know." Kim knew. She saw the equipment and crew take it out and away, but telling the little story would take a little work. It was just a whole lot easier to say "don't know."

"Any phone calls?"

"Oh, yeah. The guy from the art school called and said they approved me for a scholarship."

"How much?"

"Ten thousand, just like they said they would. Isn't that great?"

"Yeah, that's great. But, I've been thinking…"

"He said we better get right in and sign up before they decided to take it and give it to someone else. Something about a budget and all that. I didn't…"

"Look Kim, that's still twenty thousand a year, just for tuition, then there's books and stuff."

"I can get a school loan. Everyone gets school loans."

"And this is going to take four years, right? That's at least eighty thousand dollars after it's all said and done. At least."

"I can pay it back after I graduate."

"How? How you going to do that, exactly?"

"As an artist. What else? Isn't that what I'm going to school for?"

"You're talented, Kim. But I don't want for you to get your hopes up…"

"That's your trouble, mom. You don't think big and look where it's got you. Nowhere." Kim was beginning to pout. She turned away from her mother.

"All I'm saying is that if you want to be an artist, you can be an artist. I'm sure you would make a good one. But I don't think they make that much money to pay back that kind of a loan. I know I sure can't pay that kind of money. Why don't you enroll in American River? They teach art and would be a heck of a lot cheaper."

"First of all, artists do make that kind of money. Ever hear of Damien Hirst?"

"Not really."

"Well, he's made over a billion dollars, and he's not talented at all. All he does is draw big polka dots or put a dead animal in some formaldehyde, and he gets millions for that crap. I got more talent than him, believe you me. I don't see why I can't get rich if he got rich. And even if I didn't make a billion, say I just made a fraction, how much would that be? Certainly enough to pay back a measly eighty thousand."

"So what's wrong with the junior college? You haven't answered that one."

"Junior college, community college. They made a TV comedy about a community college. It's a joke. It's for losers." She gave her mother a look that said if you push me, you know I'll have to call you a loser.

"Well first you have to finish high school and graduate. I told you goofing off in those two classes was going to bite you in the rear."

"The guy from the art school said that was no big deal. If I couldn't take care of it this summer I could get a GED and start this September. No big deal. I'm going to be an artist not a scientist. Don't you get it, mom? Can't I do this? I haven't asked for much. Can't I at least have this one thing?"

"I don't even know why we're having this conversation. You're eighteen now. You can do what you want. If you want to take out the loans and go to that school, I can't stop you. You're a big girl now. But remember, the bed you make is the bed you sleep in."

"I know that. But, I'm going to need your help. I need your support. I'm going to have to live here. I can't work. I got to go to school."

"You plan on staying at home, with me, until you graduate?"

"That's the plan, Sam."

"Okay, then. You can go to that fancy art school, and you can live here. But when you're rich and famous, remember your old mom, alright?"

"Sure, mom. I'll buy you a big house someday. I love you, mom."

Kathy's heart was warmed by the "I love you, mom."

"That guy from the school, when did he say we should come in to sign the papers?"

"Oh yeah, I forgot to tell you. I made an appointment for you and me to be in his office this evening at seven. He said he was doing us a favor by seeing us so late and not to miss it because, you never know what could happen to the scholarship. That's what he said."

The admission advisor said emphatically, sitting behind his cherry wood desk, "I'm glad you're taking advantage of this opportunity. An education is something that can never be taken from you. Besides, studies show that those with a degree do so much better in life, financially speaking. And just from my own experience, they do better in all aspects of life. This is what makes my job so rewarding. This is why I get up in the morning to be part of helping you help yourself."

He went by Marc with a "c" because he thought it was ironic that the hustler was called Marc. His real name was Todd. He wore a gold Rolex knockoff. When he started out, he couldn't afford a genuine Rolex, but he figured a knockoff would do the trick. Who would know the difference? After all, he wasn't hustling jewelers. He was just hustling kids with stars in their eyes, so easy.

He wore the phony watch because he had read a book about selling that said an expensive watch should be in every salesman's tool box. The book's basic strategy was making the sale by telling the prospective customer what he or she wanted to hear and also intimidation. Not brute intimidation making someone scared that would only frighten them away, but subtle intimidation of placing the salesman on a higher social plane than the buyer, having the buyer looking up to the salesman. The same idea as having the judge in the courtroom sitting above all others, or a preacher in the pulpit. A matter of establishing the pecking order so that the buyer would submit to the salesman's will. According to the book, the social order was established by who had the most wealth. No faster way to establish that status than with an expensive watch. The kid on the playground with the most marbles was always the big shot.

He didn't have to bring attention to the gold monster on his wrist; it was as obvious as the sun at noon in Vegas. It was his talisman. He had faith in its power to push the fence sitter off and make him sign. It gave him confidence that when the dust settled, there would be a sale.

This confidence came shining through for the customer to see. It worked like a charm.

Marc worked strictly on commission, ten percent. He would make $2,000 on the $20,000 student loan Kim was about to sign. He got his check when the lender sent the funds to the school. He never sold anything more than the $20,000 golden opportunity, because every student qualified for the $10,000 scholarship. Who could turn down saving $10,000 even if it meant going in debt for $20,000.

Kathy didn't need to cosign the loan documents. Kim had just turned eighteen, which triggered the phone call for her to get down to his office before she lost her chance of a lifetime. California presumed that by her age she was mature enough to fully understand her rights and obligations under the contract she would shortly enter.

Of course Marc didn't explain any of her obligations. The book said tell the buyer what he wants to hear. Kim didn't want to hear that there was no relief from a student loan, no filing bankruptcy, or that she was on her way to becoming a debt slave with accumulating interest. Her high school didn't teach her any of these lessons either. Their message was more like "go to college and everything is going to be hunky-dory."

Kim signed all the papers. There was a cooling off period of seventy-two hours when Kim could back out for no reason, which was printed on the back of the contract. After that, the trap's steel jaws would slam shut. Since she could back out in the next three days, Marc was still laying on the charm. He knew that he had put her in a trance and wanted to keep her asleep, having a dream about her future. He congratulated them on making the decision to take the giant step forward. Showing them out, he opened his office door for them as if they were a queen and a princess.

In the car, going back to their apartment they stopped off at a pie shop to celebrate with coconut cream pie and ice cream.

Over their deserts, Kathy asked Kim, "What did you think of Marc? Wasn't he nice?"

"Nice isn't the word for it. If I could find a man like him, I would make him marry me. I don't know what he was saying. It was like I was in a trance" Kim gushed.

"Maybe you'll meet someone like that at art school. You never know."

When they got back to their apartment, the light on the answering machine was on, flashing. Kathy pushed the play button.

"Kathy, this is Janet from the office. Don't go over to Mr. Spader's tomorrow. Come directly to the office. There's been a change, and I'll talk to you about it tomorrow morning. Be in the office by nine. Okay, see you then. Bye."

Kim asked, "What's that about?"

"Don't know. Maybe my patient died and they don't need me now. Sounds like it. They'll have someone else for me. At any rate, I can sleep in a couple hours. I need it. I'm beat."

At nine sharp, Kathy was sitting in Janet's office. Janet was the owner/manager of We Totally Care. Janet had built up the business from scratch. She realized that her employees were her most valuable asset, and her only other asset was her reputation. She looked at her workers as money makers, each one had value in that regards, but no one was irreplaceable. The same way a dairy farmer looks at his cows. But those who Janet had to cull, from time to time, didn't wind up in McDonalds between a hamburger bun.

Looking at Kathy's personnel file, avoiding direct eye contact, Janet said, "I got a phone call from Mr. Spader last night. He was very upset."

Kathy said, "Yeah, I know. We talked. He said he wanted me to be ready to go right at seven. To get organized on my own time before that. I said I would, no problem. I don't know why…"

"It's not about that."

"Is he complaining about my car leaking a little oil on the street? He always has something to complain about."

"More serious. Very serious. He said that his father's Vicodin is missing, and that you have stolen it."

Kathy was shocked. "What? That's crazy. You know I don't use drugs."

"Would you be willing to take a drug test?"

"Yes, of course."

Janet had just said that to see what Kathy's response would be, to see if she was hiding something. Actually she believed Kathy, but that was beside the point.

"That won't be necessary," Janet said.

Kathy breathed a little sigh of relief, but Janet knew before Kathy came in that morning what she was going to do. Janet had already made up her mind.

Kathy said, "How could he say such a thing?"

"He told me that when he left in the morning there were two containers of Vicodin in his father's room. One that had a few pills and another that was full. Know anything about that?"

"I saw only one container. The one that was partially full. There were about a dozen pills in it. I know that because Richard asked for a couple while I was there and I gave him the container. You know we're not supposed to give them their med's directly, and I don't."

"Well, he said when he got home and checked in on his father, the full container was missing. And since you were the only one in the house, you must have taken the Vicodin. Was there anyone else in the house that could have taken the pills, like a repairman, a cable guy, or somebody?"

"No. Me and Richard were the only ones there. Did he look around real good? Could they be somewhere else, like under the bed or somewhere?"

"I asked him that, and he said he had looked but didn't find them."

Janet was lying. She never asked Mr. Spader that question. She didn't defend Kathy either. She didn't tell Mr. Spader that Kathy had worked for We Totally Care for the past seven years with never a complaint or allegation against her integrity, much less stealing. But Janet did listen to Mr. Spader who said he would go on Yelp and give a horrible review, including the incident of stolen Vicodin, if We Totally Care didn't fire Kathy. He ended his threat with saying he wasn't being vindictive but was just trying to protect those in the future from the same thing happening to them.

Janet liked Kathy. She had been a good worker. She was always on time, and didn't call in sick, or have some other reason why she couldn't work. She had made a lot of money off of her over the last seven years. But she knew Mr. Spader wasn't bluffing, and she didn't want any trouble from him that could damage the reputation of We Totally Care, especially the accusation of a caregiver stealing a narcotic. Kathy would have to go. Finding a replacement would be easy; Janet had more than enough job applications on file.

Janet handed Kathy her last check, wished her good luck, and escorted her out the door.

Kathy was stunned when she left the office. Being in a daze, she nearly got hit by another car when she went through a red light. By the time she got home, the stunned feeling gave way to hurt. She opened up the refrigerator and self-medicated with a half-gallon of rocky road ice cream.

Kathy didn't waste any time looking for a new job. She lived from paycheck to paycheck. She needed to find a life line and grab it, or else she would drown in the sea of poverty. She had a fear of being thrown out of her apartment and having to live in her car. The first day of job hunting wasn't successful. Filling out the applications, there was always one question that scared her, the question that read, "Have you ever been dismissed from employment? If so, please explain." She answered the question "yes" and explained that she was unjustly accused of something she didn't do. She didn't get into details. She didn't lie and say no. She was proud that she wasn't a liar. Lying was against the Ten Commandments. Besides, all they had to do was make a phone call to We Totally Care, and they would find out she had been fired. Then how would that look, a liar, a thief, a drug addict. But, so far, she didn't get an interview and chance to fully explain.

If she didn't get a job with her twenty years of experience as an in-home caregiver, she would try the convalescent hospitals. This is what she told herself, but she had a bad feeling, a deep feeling that she was doomed.

Kathy and Kim were on the couch eating ice cream, drinking Mountain Dew.

"Have any luck today?"

"No. Not yet. But something will turn up. Say, Kim, I want you to start looking for a job."

"Mom, I can't. I'm in school. You know I don't have time for a job."

"A part time job. Doesn't have to be full time. A lot of kids work while they're in school. I used to work while I was in school."

"And where exactly, where am I supposed to find a job? Where?" Kim threw her hands up in the air as if it was impossible to find something.

Kathy's stress had shortened her rope. She had come to the end of it. She exploded, "Damn it, Kimberley. I need your help. I lost my job. Don't you understand? We've got no money coming in. There's no money in the bank except in the checking account, and the bills keep coming in, Kim. We've got about thirty days, and then the manager is going to throw us out, and you're going to have to go live with your father!"

"Not my fault you got fired! Don't blame me!" Kim shouted back.

"I'm not blaming you. I just need your help. I need you to get a damn job and start contributing! Bring in some money for Pete's sake!"

"Not my job, mom. And if we do get evicted, so what? We'll just find another place."

"With what, Kim? Don't you get it, damn it! You think money grows on trees or something?"

"I'll go live with dad then, and stop cussing at me."

Kathy sat there fuming. Her face was beet red. She got up and walked over to get her bag hanging on the door knob. She sat down in a deep green, velour easy chair. She opened her bag and found the papers from the art school. She read the cancellation clause. Tomorrow was the deadline for canceling.

"Tomorrow you're going with me to see what's his name."

"You mean Marc?"

"Yeah, Marc."

Kathy had called the admissions office about canceling over the phone. She wasn't eager about making a trip over to the school and having to do it in person. The clerk insisted that the cancellation, in order to be valid, had to be in writing and delivered by the end of the day. Kathy coerced Kim into signing a cancellation letter. What did the trick was the threat of Kim immediately going to live with her father if she didn't sign. Kim didn't want to live with him because he would insist that she work. She was tired of having him say, "There's no such thing as a free lunch." When they got to the school, the admissions clerk, a young woman with a nose ring and tattoos, looked at the cancellation letter and said, "Before I can log this in, you have to see Marc. School policy. He's right down the hall."

Kathy didn't waste her breath arguing with the clerk. She could see the game they were playing. Now, she wasn't playing. Being a single mother didn't weaken her, it just made her stronger. She put on her armor of God and marched down the hall to Marc's office. She told Kim, "Watch and learn." The door to his office was open.

"Ladies, how nice to see you. Would you like a cup of coffee, tea, or something?" Marc knew why they were here. He could read it on Kathy's determined face. It was a fifty-fifty chance he could save the sale and keep his commission. The gracious welcome was just step one in the process.

"No thank you. The clerk said we had to see you first. We want to cancel."

"Cancel? Cancel? Why would you want to do that? You're throwing away a ten thousand dollar scholarship. Do you realize the strings I had to pull to get Donna that scholarship?"

"We appreciate that. It's Kim, not Donna."

"Yes, Kim. Did I say Donna? Pardon me. I was just thinking about my own daughter. Her name is Donna. He held up a family photo of him, his wife, his boy and girl. He was in the back of the group with a beaming smile and his protective arms around them. But, actually it wasn't his family. He had photo shopped it, another tool in his tool box. "You know I would make any sacrifice for her and my son, for their future. You know how it is being a good parent. What else is there, right?"

Kathy also reached in her tool box. She shouted, "We want to cancel! Do you hear me? We want to cancel!"

"Alright, alright." Marc threw in the towel. He had to get them out of his office before Kathy caused more of a scene and his boss came in. "Go back to the clerk and cancel then. But when she's stuck in some lousy job, don't blame me. I tried to help you. I really did. But some people are born losers."

"Come on, Kim. We're finished here." Kathy held her head up, turned and walked out of the office. Mommy lion led her cub down the hall.

"We saw Marc. Here's the cancellation. There better not be any more run around. You hear me?"

"The clerk whispered, "I heard. Good for you. Let me date stamp it and make you a copy. Be sure not to lose it. You never know."

The respect given by the clerk healed the pain of Marc calling her a loser. Kathy felt relieved and like a million bucks.

On the way back, they stopped off at their favorite pie shop for some, what else, pie and ice cream. Kim had chocolate cream, and Kathy had strawberry with extra whipped cream.

"Now what did you think of Marc?"

"Oh him?" Kim said it the way a girl would remark about a boyfriend who had dumped her a year ago.

"Yeah, him."

"Did you see his face when you shouted at him, 'We want to cancel'?" Kim made a face as if she was shouting at the top of her lungs.

"He sure dropped his phony mask, so we could really see who he was. Big phony. All he wanted was the money."

"He had a nice family, though."

"Just more tricks from him to get us to like him. Don't you see…"

"Do you think he was right about being stuck in some lousy job for the rest of my life?"

"No, honey. But look, you don't need them for a good job. You can enroll in American River College. I hear they have an excellent art department. Then after two years, you can transfer to Sac State and get your degree."

"But, Mom…"

"Listen Kim, it's good to have dreams. But sometimes, dreams are just wishful thinking. You and I aren't the type of people destined to be rich and famous. It's not going to happen. We were made to work hard for what little we get. Don't mean to kill your dreams, but that's reality. If you want to study art, that's fine if you couple it with someday being a teacher - something that can make you a living. You know your grandma was a great painter. She even sold some, but I saw how hard it was for her, even with her talent. She made about enough to pay for her paint and canvass and very little for her time."

"But there are artists who make millions. You know how much some of those paintings of Pollock go for?"

"I don't know anything about whoever you mentioned. But I know you. It's not your destiny. You're not going to get rich as an artist. You just won't."

"You never know."

"You're right. You never know until you try. This is what I want you to do while you're going to school. I want you to try and sell your art. I want you to learn for yourself what it's like to make it as an artist. While the teachers are teaching you how to draw and paint, let the world teach you what it's like to make a living off of it. I'll bet they don't teach you that sort of thing in any art school."

"And how am I supposed to work, go to school, and sell my art?"

"Okay, you win. For the first year you don't have to work. Just go to school, do your art, and try to sell it. Okay?"

"What about getting evicted and all that? I thought I had to work so we wouldn't be homeless."

"Let me worry about that. This afternoon, I'm going to look for a job at the convalescent hospitals by us. They're always hiring. People come and go."

"You shouldn't say 'worry.' You know what the pastor was preaching about last Sunday, about words and how powerful they are."

"You're right. Forgive me, Lord. I meant to say, I'll take care of that."

She was feeling relieved that the future debt of $20,000 had been lifted. Even if her daughter was on the hook for the money, she knew she would be the one paying off the loan, not her daughter. Her victory over Marc had given her a shot of energy to her sagging self-confidence. Nothing like a battle to get her juices flowing.

Two young men from Hospital Supply Co. were at Mr. Spader's house. They were taking away the hospital bed Richard had used. He had died a couple weeks after Kathy got fired.

"Don't scratch the floor. I had these hardwood floors installed not that long ago. I don't want any scratches on them. Can you carry it instead of rolling it?" Mr. Spader complained.

"This thing is built like a tank, all iron." The younger guy had a complaint of his own.

"We're going to have to turn it on its side to get it through the door." The older one supervised.

"How did I wind up with the end with the motor again? Every time I get the motor. You know how heavy this motor is?"

Normally the two guys didn't do any complaining, just get in and get out. Half the time they were at a pickup because the patient didn't make it, and they didn't want to be disrespectful to the relatives with a lot of whining. The family had enough grief of their own. But Mr. Spader had set the tone by complaining that they were fifteen minutes late and complained about everything since. It was only noon and it was already one hundred with the temperature rising. On top of that, the truck's air conditioning wasn't working.

When they got the bed out of the spare bedroom and on the way to the truck, Mr. Spader noticed an amber plastic container on the floor where the bed had been. He picked it up and read the label, "Vicodin." It was full.

Mr. Spader realized what had happened. It had fallen on the floor somehow, rolled across the floor, and wound up behind one of the bed wheels. Mr. Spader unscrewed the cap, looked inside, shook the pills, then screwed the cap back on. He wondered if he could get a refund from the pharmacy, but it never occurred to him that he should call We Totally Care and admit his mistake, to try to get Kathy her job back. He had made his final payment to We Totally Care. He was finished with them.

The empty bedroom was terribly sad. A mixture of sadness and relief came over Mr. Spader. He looked at the Vicodin, unscrewed the cap, and swallowed a pill. He thought it would help numb the pain he was feeling. He didn't think one would hurt. A couple hours later, he took another.

Three weeks had gone by and Kathy had not been out on one job interview. She was at the end of her rope. She thought the question asking if she had ever been fired was putting the kibosh on finding work. She was looking for a loophole for not having to tell the truth about her work history. She thought the pastor of her small church would give his blessing for her to tell a little white lie considering the circumstances, that is, she was innocent of what she was accused, and she was getting real close to the wolf knocking on her door.

Kathy sat in Pastor Jerry's office, telling her story about how she came to get fired. The pastor gave all the necessary facial expressions to let her know that he believed her and was appalled at the injustice of her being fired. He told himself to focus while Kathy droned on, going into way too much detail in a monotone. He fought back the urge to yawn. At the end of her story, he thought about how much her job loss was going to cost him in collections and what it was going to cost him to help her: probably a couple sacks of groceries out of the food closet, and of course he would tell her that she would be in his prayers. He hated this part of the job, having to listen to people's problems.

"That's terrible, Kathy, what happened to you. Wish you would have come to see me a lot earlier. How exactly can I help you?"

"Well Pastor Jerry, I need some guidance. I'm confused."

Here it comes, he thought. She's going to tell me that she has tithed, now she's broke and wants an explanation.

Kathy didn't even consider telling him that she had been a faithful tither and felt cheated by the whole fiasco. Privately she mulled the fact that she had given and given happily ten percent and not just of the net, but of her gross pay, and look what the outcome was. Instead of being blessed, she felt cursed.

"How so?" the pastor asked.

"Well, on all the job questionnaires it asks, have you been dismissed, and if so, explain. I feel like I'm getting penalized for being an honest person. I tell the truth and not even getting an interview. If I came up with some story, I could at least get a job interview. Once I was on the job, they would see how good of a worker I was and keep me on, even if they later found out I got fired. What do you think?"

"That would probably get you a job, yes."

"So it's okay if I tell a little fib then?"

Pastor Jerry's mind flashed on how the Pharisees had tried to trap Jesus with tricky questions. He didn't have any original answers for this riddle of morality, but he had the time-proven clichés that had been used by pastors for centuries. "You know that we are called to pick up our cross and follow Him."

"Yeah, but I didn't do anything wrong in the first place."

"Neither did He, and look what happened to Him. He understands your suffering. He has been there himself. I know you are going through a lot right now, but He went through a whole lot worse."

Kathy could see that it wasn't going to do her any good trying to convince him to give his blessing concerning the fib. She felt disappointed, a feeling she was getting used to. She just wanted to leave and get back to looking for a job.

"Have you filed for unemployment?"

"No point. I can't get it if I was fired. And, besides, even if I could get it, by the time I got my first check I would be living in my car."

"No savings?"

She felt like telling him that it went into the collection plate, but she didn't. When she was a kid and got sassy, her mother would smack her, so she learned to curb her rapier wit. "No, afraid not."

"Well, I can give you a couple sacks of groceries, if that would help."

"From the food closet?"

"Yes."

"Thanks for the offer, but my self-respect is about the only thing I've got left. You see this tattoo on my arm. Even it is fading away." She had "Kim" tattooed on her upper arm.

"Kathy, you're a care giver. You've always been a care giver. That's the first thing I saw in you. And that's a wonderful thing. I think women have much more of that in them than men. Wasn't it the women who took care of Jesus? Wasn't it the women who went to the tomb to take care of his sacred body? But, the thing is, you have to learn to receive as well as give. Maybe that's what this whole thing is about. The Lord is teaching you a lesson. He just might be teaching you to receive as well as give. I'm a care giver too. I know it's difficult to accept people's help. The scripture says that it's more blessed to give than to receive. But I've found that it's more difficult to receive. For me, it's my doggone pride that gets in the way. You know pride is one of the seven deadly sins and maybe the worst. I've been fighting my own pride ever since I turned my life over to the Lord." Pastor Jerry liked the preaching and pontificating part of the job. He thought of himself as being a wise man.

Kathy got up to go. "We've got enough groceries to hold us for a while, but if we run out, I'll take you up on your offer."

Pastor Jerry got up from behind his desk as well. "Yes, of course. Don't hesitate to come in and get what you need. But we have a policy of just two bags a week. You understand. And how is your daughter?"

"Kim is doing fine. She's graduating finally and enrolling at American River College."

"I'm sure you're very proud of her."

"Oh, I am."

As he was showing her out, he said, "I'll keep you in my prayers."

Later that night as Pastor Jerry was getting ready for bed, he said his nightly prayers, but Kathy wasn't mentioned. He found praying for others laborious.

Kathy usually prayed once she got into bed. If she didn't, she couldn't get to sleep. This night she prayed kneeling beside her bed. She prayed with all her might, first whispering words of praise and thanksgiving. Then she beseeched her God for His help in finding a job that would meet her financial needs, give her an outlet for sharing her gifts with others, and where she would be treated fairly. After her prayer she kept her eyes closed, waiting to see a vision or hear God's voice. There was only darkness and silence, but in her spirit she could sense someone silently listening to her. She let her tears flow, got into bed, and fell into a deep sleep. She was completely empty and open. She had a dream that night of herself baking and eating bread.

When Kathy woke up she thought she would check out the hospitals in the area to see if they were hiring. Maybe it would be a step up in benefits and pay. After Kim got off the computer, checking her Facebook page, it was Kathy's turn. Yes, a couple of the hospitals, Mercy and Kaiser, were looking for orderlies. Why didn't she think of this before? Being an orderly in a hospital was the same work she was doing before, just not at the patient's home. The only bugaboo was the same as everywhere else, the question about "have you ever been dismissed." She filled out the application on the line truthfully. At least she didn't have to waste her time driving down there to hear the same thing "we'll contact you."

"Mom, have you tried Craigslist?" Kim asked.

"What's that?"

"Craigslist. It's like what the want ads or the Penney Saver used to be. Remember the Penney Saver?"

"Oh, yeah. The good ol' days," Kathy said. "How come you know about the Penney Saver and the want ads? We don't take a paper."

"We were talking about it in class yesterday, about how the internet has changed everything. Check it out. See if there's a job in there."

Kathy started pecking on the keyboard, finding Craigslist, checking out the site, from one category to the next. "This is amazing. Like a huge community bulletin board at the supermarket. They got everything on here. How much does it cost to put an ad in?"

Kim came over and stood behind her mother, looking over her shoulder at the site. "Nothing. It's free."

"Free! No way!"

"Yes way."

"How do they make money then?"

"Don't know."

"So this is what killed the Penney Saver. Haven't seen it for years, wondered what happened to it."

"Helped kill the papers, too."

"I can see why. They used to make a lot of money off those ads. I thought about putting an ad in the paper once but it was too expensive. They wanted over thirty dollars for just a couple days. I figured the ad would eat up all my profits."

"For what?"

"What'a ya' mean, 'for what'?"

"What did you want the ad for?"

"I was thinking of starting my own business, care giving."

"Mom! Why don't you put an ad in now on Craigslist? It's free, not going to do any harm, not like it's going to cost you something."

"Out of the mouths of babes. Can you do it for me? I'll tell you what to say."

"Sure, Mom. Move then, and let me sit down."

Kathy got excited composing the ad. The feeling of hope was overwhelming. She called her new company Kathy's In-Home Care Company. She spelled out company rather than abbreviating it because to her it sounded more professional. She stated that she had over twenty years of experience, was a good cook, would furnish references, competitive fees. She listed her cell phone number because she understood that promptness was very important. It took about fifteen minutes, and she was in business.

"Thanks, Kim. I couldn't have done it without you."

Kim beamed a little with pride. "Oh, that's okay. You want to go get some pie or something?"

"Yeah, I would but later. Right now I got work to do. I got to look in my address book of former clients and give them a call to see if I can use them as references."

Kathy sent out Christmas cards to the clients that she had a fondness for. The ones like Mr. Spader didn't get a card. The first person she called was Ralph Leer. She had taken care of his mother who was bedridden for several years before dying. Ralph and his wife were both retired after turning their Ford dealership over to their two sons. They were at home most of the time while Kathy was in the house looking after Ralph's mother and knew Kathy quite well. They gave her a generous cash gift when his mother died in appreciation for the care Kathy had given her.

Kathy let the phone ring several times and was about to hang up when Ralph Leer answered, "Hello." His voice sounded a little tired and a little worried.

"Mr. Leer, this is Kathy. How are you?"

"Well, Kathy," his voice became a little lighter, a little cheerful, "how are you? You won't believe this, but I was just thinking of you. My mother-in-law, Darlene's mother, was in the hospital, then in the convalescent hospital for a couple weeks, and now she's coming to live with us. I was just about ready to call that company, what's its name, and ask for you."

"When will she be getting out of the convalescent hospital and living with you?"

"Tomorrow."

"I don't work for that company anymore. I've got my own business now."

"Oh, I see. You got people working for you?"

"Not yet. I've just started it, and right now it's just me."

"Can you take care of her? I'll pay the same unless you want a little more. Payday would be every Friday. How does that sound? I would need you here just for five days a week. On the weekends Darlene and I can take care of her on our own."

"The same amount would be fine. When do you want me to start?"

"Well, she's supposed to be here tomorrow morning about ten. I'm going to pick her up and bring her over, but things like this always take longer than you expect. How about noon? You can start by cooking her one of your tasty lunches. How's that?"

"I'll be at your house right at twelve, okay?"

"Fine. Okay, we'll see you tomorrow. I'm glad you called. You took a load off my mind. Now I know that I've got someone reliable to look after her. It must have been fate or something that you called."

"Yes, must have been fate or something. I'll see you then. Bye." Kathy waited for him to hang up, and then she hung up her phone.

Kim said, "I heard. That's awesome!"

"Telling me? And he's paying me the same as what he used to pay We Totally Care, which means I'll be making a lot more, and payday starts this Friday. Thank you, Lord! Yes, thank you, Lord! Let's go celebrate with some pie and ice cream."

Two Sacks of Groceries

Highway 89 was closed because of the fire, so I took 88 all the way into Minden, which put me behind schedule. I had to get the key to the cabin by six o'clock or else wind up sleeping in my truck for the night. There was time but it would be cutting it thin.

I was in Bishop by 4:30, plenty of time to get a Number One combo at Carl's Jr. Rolling down the truck window, the 103 degree heat hit me in the face. In a while, I would be at the 10,000 foot elevation where everything would be comfortably warm, rather than scorching hot. "Have a nice day," I said to the teenager at the drive thru window as I drove away and onto Main Street, heading south down memory lane.

A couple lights later, I turned west on Line Street. At this corner of Main and Line is where my Uncle Joe and Aunt Margie had their liquor store, Joe's Liquor. When I was in high school, I would come up for a week, either on the Greyhound or drive up in my pickup, and spend some time working in the store, stocking and rotating the cases of beer and soda in the walk-in cooler, getting paid with a candy bar. I thought the candy bar was something generous - I appreciated it - since I never expected to get paid by a family member for helping out a little. My aunt and uncle showed me love because they didn't have any kids, and I was there for just a week. Besides, I never complained about anything, certainly not lending a hand.

The liquor store was a magical place with an ice machine that never ran out of ice cubes, shelves stocked with boxes of candy bars, packs of Lucky cigarettes throwing off their sweet scent, green and amber glass bottles of whiskey with strange names like Cutty Sark and Old Crow. Regulars and tourists would come into the store, and I would sell them what they wanted. Looking back, I guess we were breaking the law because I wasn't even shaving then, but back in the day folks weren't hung up on technicalities. This was before the nannies started laying down the law.

Some customers had credit and would pay when they got their check at the end of the month. This gave my uncle a competitive edge because the grocery stores, which also sold beer and liquor, wouldn't give anyone credit. So those who liked cold beer on a hot day but didn't have the cash could get a case or six pack down at Joe's Liquor. Uncle Joe kept tab on a customer's credit on a 3 by 5 card, which he kept in a little, tin recipe box. One time while I was in the store, a couple drunks came in, and one wanted to pay his tab and buy some beer. When my uncle told him how much he owed, the drunk said, "I didn't get that much beer! I don't owe you that much!"

"Yes you did," my uncle said, looking the drunk in the eye.

"No I didn't!"

"Alright then! You don't want to pay what you owe, get out! No more credit!" he said, tearing up the guy's tab and throwing it in the trashcan. Uncle Joe didn't mess around. He never was held up, and I pity the guy who would try.

Both my aunt and uncle would sell to anyone who was over 21 whether they were sober or drunk. They weren't there in the store to be life coaches; they just wanted to ring the cash register, not tell someone how to live. Neither my aunt nor my uncle drank much, not even bothering to keep it around the house.

All the locals knew my uncle Joe, and he knew everyone. When he and I would walk around town, say go over to the Chinese restaurant, The Hong Kong Café, for a plate of chop suey, folks in their cars would holler, "Hey, Joe!"

Uncle Joe would holler back, "Hey, Charlie!" or "So, sue me!" He liked saying "so sue me" a lot. He was the quintessential, independent, small business man asking nothing of anyone, except to be left alone so he could do his thing.

When two in the morning came around, he would lock up, and we would go over to Schat's bakery, which was just a little hole in the wall before they built their fancy bakery. Joe would go in there and pick up some fresh sheepherder's bread. The aroma of flour, yeast, and baking bread would welcome us. The bakers, wearing white pants and white t-shirts, would be at their table kneading dough by hand, throwing loose flour around generously to keep the dough from sticking to the work surface. The bakers were doing something for a living that was incredible - making our daily bread. Uncle Joe would chat with them, usually about the Dodgers, while he picked up a loaf of fresh bread, but never making himself a nuisance with too much small talk. My uncle never gossiped; he was too busy pursuing happiness. The bakers were busy working, not gabbing, building a famous bakery. Uncle Joe was a special person in Bishop; he was the only one who could go into the bakery at 2:30 in the morning and get his bread. Once he got what he needed, we were off in his old Cadillac back to the house.

Marge and Joe had a small house about five miles out of town on Bishop creek, which with the help of my granddad, they built by themselves. It was this opportunity of living on the creek that drew them up from San Bernardino right after WWII to one of the most scenic places on Earth. Out of the living room window, they could see the High Sierras rising straight up from the valley floor. The mountain peaks were all nearly 14,000 feet high with snow on their summits year round. Looking the other direction across the valley, they could see clearly the White Mountains, also capped with snow, on the Nevada border. From the kitchen window, they could look out on Bishop Creek, which supplied them with fresh, cold water. At night, if you listened for it, you could hear the creek singing its constant hymn of praise to the Creator of all this beauty.

I used to love fishing in the creek. My uncle taught me the tricks: how to tie the right knot, the proper sinker for different water conditions. We would use salmon eggs, nothing fancy. A jar of eggs bought at Mac's Sporting Goods a few shops up from the liquor store, with its beautiful neon sign of a rainbow trout, would last the week. I knew every rock and every riffle where I could count on finding either a rainbow or a small native brown. For browns, worms were best. If I wasn't at the store, sweeping the floor or stocking the cooler, I was on the creek fishing. Could heaven been better?

They got this property, where the nearest neighbor was about a quarter mile down the dirt road, from the City of Los Angeles as a lifelong lease that would expire when they died or moved away. The City of Los Angeles acquired a lot of this land by getting President Hoover to renege on a treaty with the Native Americans, the Paiutes, who had been living along the creek for about nine thousand years. The US Government had originally set aside 67,000 acres for the Paiute reservation, but President Hoover in 1936 took most of the land and gave it to Los Angeles, leaving only 875 acres for the Paiute tribe. Los Angeles wanted the land for the water. Why they leased property to my aunt and uncle was never explained to me.

After my uncle would wake up, he would have his morning coffee and look at the L.A. Times. He and I would sit in the living room with its open beam ceiling and fireplace made out of rocks found on the property. Beautiful oil paintings of the mountains and creek, painted by my grandma, hung on the walls. A large braided rug made out of wool scraps, also made by grandma, was on the floor. Homemade furniture from weathered gray boards served as a coffee table and end tables. We would talk about baseball and the stock market. To me the stock market was the most interesting. Uncle Joe was following Anaconda Copper and a Cuban sugar company that went kaput when Castro took over. He wasn't the best at picking stocks, and, as time would tell, neither was I. Politics and religion were never discussed. I thought it unusual that they didn't go to church but never mentioned it to them.

Eventually my aunt and uncle sold their liquor store. Uncle Joe lived for several years after that, working part time for Bishop spraying mosquitoes in the summer. One day he had a heart attack, and my aunt found his body in the creek he loved so much. My aunt continued to live in the house without him, but moved away to Arizona in her eighties to be closer to a surviving sister, where she too died.

Once my aunt and uncle were no longer in the house, the City of Los Angeles took back the property and bulldozed the house, leaving nothing behind, not even the rocks from the fireplace. An apple tree and plum tree, which they had planted, were the only silent survivors to give testimony that Aunt Margie and Uncle Joe once lived here. Their presence on the creek faded just like the presence of the Paiutes.

On this day, on my way to the cabin, I would be passing where my aunt and uncle lived. I thought it would be a good idea to make a slight detour to their place and pick up some firewood. I would need the wood for cooking and to build a cheerful campfire for the night.

I pulled off West Line and onto Otey Rd. A woman in a SUV was turning onto Line as I was turning onto Otey. Sometimes the locals would go up to where the house used to be and party there, leaving a mess of trash behind. I was hoping no one was there. The old home site was about a quarter mile up the dirt road. I drove past the neighbor's abandoned singlewide mobile home that had been set on fire since the last time I was here. Around the trailer were seventy years of abandoned cars and trucks that stopped running a long time ago and sat there, paint fading in the constant sun. A half ton of broken glass from beer and wine bottles lied on the ground with sun glare reflecting off the shards. The background for this trash heap was the majestic Sierras, with just a touch of snow trying to hang on before global warming melted the last patch in the shade.

"Good! There's no one here, no cars, nobody," I thought. I pulled my white Toyota Tundra into the shade under a cottonwood tree. I got out, and the sun's heat and babbling creek welcomed me. No house, no aunt, no uncle, not even their dog Toby was there. The emptiness made me feel a little melancholy. "Life goes on," I thought.

I put down the tailgate, sat on it, and ate my cheeseburger, fries and drank my Coke. I washed my hands and face in the creek. Yes, things have changed, but the creek was the same. It was still crystal clear, cold, and singing its song, the same song of joy and praise I had heard as a boy.

I got busy collecting firewood. Someone had sawed down a huge cottonwood. They took the main trunk and large branches, leaving behind scraps. What they wanted with a cottonwood, who knows? It's a great wood for carving, which is what the Hopi use for carving kachina dolls. They say it's easy to work, not too hard and doesn't split. If that's why they wanted the tree, it would last a lifetime of carving because it was a huge tree. I was after the scraps since they were just the right size for a fire and had been sitting in the sun for a few years, dry as a bone, able to catch fire with a single match. It was an excellent wood for barbequing, adding a mild, woody, smoky flavor to the meat.

While I was picking up wood, I heard this woman's voice, "Sir. Sir."

I looked around, and a woman was poking her head out from behind a willow. She looked like she was forty-something with peroxide blonde hair. Her eyes wandered from corner to corner, like the eyes of a cheap teddy bear you would win at the carnival. Her story of a hard life was written on her face.

"What the heck?" I thought, "Where did she come from?" Bishop was about four miles down the road, and the closest house with anyone living in it might have been a mile away. "Hi," I said.

She came out from behind the willows and stood about ten yards in front of me, wearing a t-shirt, red shorts, and flip-flops. "Are you going into Bishop?" she asked.

"No, I'm going the other way, up the canyon."

"You aren't going to Brown's Campground?" she asked. She saw the Brown's sticker on my windshield from the last time I was in Bishop a couple months ago. The campground was on the edge of Bishop.

"No, I'm going up to Parcher's."

"Where's Parcher's?"

"Parcher's Resort. It's up the canyon, that way," I said, pointing with a piece of wood.

"Oh," she said. "Can you give me a ride into Bishop? I got a couple sacks of groceries, and they're real heavy."

I thought, "Okay, this is the part where the boyfriend jumps out and hits me over the head and robs me. Caution! On the other hand, it's 103 degrees out here, and it's a long walk into town. But I don't have that much time to be driving around, playing the Good Samaritan. I've got to be at the cabin before the office closes. It's 103."

"Can you?" she asked again.

"Sure. I'll give you a ride, but first I got to collect some firewood."

"Well, I'll get started then. I'll get started walking down the road," she told me.

I thought, "You could just wait for me. I'll be done in a few minutes. Save yourself a walk in this heat. Besides, walking isn't going to get you there any sooner." But, I let her do what she wanted to do.

Apparently she had made some earlier bright decision that got her stranded in the middle of nowhere, so why ruin her day by doing something that made sense.

It didn't take long to get all the firewood I needed, just a few minutes. It was lying about everywhere. I thought, "If I ask her to sit in the back of the truck bed, she would get offended. If she fell out of the back or bumped her head, she would sue me. I guess I better move some of my stuff out of the front seat and make room for her." I put a travel bag and pillow in the back seat, and left the Keurig coffee maker in the middle of the front seat, separating our space.

Driving down the dirt road, I didn't see her. I thought, "Good. She caught a ride. Don't have to worry about her." Then I saw her at the end of the road. "Darn! There she is. She must be strong, got down to the end of the road awfully fast." I drove down to the end of Otey Rd. where it intersects the two lane highway, and she was standing in the shade of a small tree with her two, brown paper, grocery bags, talking on her cellphone. I looked around for the boyfriend, who would also want a ride, but there wasn't one, and there was no place for one to hide, jumping out from a rock at the last second. I leaned over and swung the door open for her to get in.

She looked a little peeved about the Keurig taking up some of the room. She made a couple trips back and forth, picking up her two sacks of groceries, baguette of bread sticking out of one, talking on the phone the whole time. She said to whomever was on the phone, "Yeah, I've got a ride. I'll have him drop me off at Karen's...."

She finally got her grocery bags in the truck, still talking on the phone, "Well, it costs seven dollars, and I've got five so far....Yeah, I'm crowd funding....He's so cool...He google plused me...."

I was waiting for her to buckle on her safety belt, looking forward to finding out from her how she managed to wind up in the middle of nowhere with two sacks of groceries on a blistering hot, summer day. But, before we could get moving, she said, "There's my ride!" pointing to a small, white, county shuttle bus on the other side of the highway. "I'm going to catch the bus." She mimed saying "thank you" to me and kept the phone up to her ear. She got out and took her two grocery bags with her. As soon as she was out of the truck, and her door was shut closed, I turned left and headed up the canyon. I felt relieved as I looked in my rearview mirror and watched her cross the road to catch her bus. I thought, "She's good at carrying groceries; didn't break a bag, and they weren't even double bagged."

Maurice Utrillo - Making Do

I read all the books about Maurice Utrillo, French 20th century cityscape painter, that I could find in our public library. I even read the biography of his mother, Suzanne Valadon. I remember thinking when I read his story, "This man could have been autistic." One of his biographers said that when he had dinner with him, the only thing Utrillo would say was, "How tall are you?" The biographer would tell him and Utrillo would say, "That's tall." A little while later, "How tall are you?"

He was a troubled kid. His mother took him to a doctor for help. The wise doctor said, "Why don't you teach him to paint? You know how to paint. That'll keep him occupied and out of trouble." He made do with his mother's instruction. Painting kept him occupied for the next 50 plus years, painting thousands of pictures. They're in museums today. She gave him a limited palette, less expensive paint. He made do. His best works were from this simple palette, what they call his "white period." In the beginning, he and his mother didn't have money for canvass. He used cardboard. He made do until he could afford canvass.

His painting set him free from poverty, but the painting couldn't set him free from alcohol. He was a teenage alcoholic and addicted until the day he died. He would get drunk, get frustrated, and someone would beat him up. When people hassled him painting on the street, he made do by copying post cards in his studio. A couple times the authorities locked him up in a mental institution because of his addiction. A third time rap would have sent him away for life. In the mental pen, in his small room, he continued to paint. He made do. His mother didn't know for sure who his father was, so one of her boyfriends, Utrillo, said Maurice could take his name. Even with his name he had to make do.

I was in Paris, in Montmartre, Utrillo's old stomping grounds. I was on my way to Saint Vincent Cemetery to put a rose on Utrillo's grave. When I got there, the cemetery keeper was heading out and putting a padlock on the gate. The sign on the cemetery gate noted that it closed at 6 p.m. I had ten minutes left. A man and a woman were waiting for the keeper. It looked like the three of them were in a hurry to get to a restaurant or a bar. I pointed to the time on the sign. The woman got a frown on her face, and the keeper shook his head "no." My polite protest didn't do any good. "I'll be back," I said. The woman got her smile back, and the keeper shrugged as if to say "whatever."

I walked around the corner of the cemetery, up the cobbled stone Rue des Saules. What to do with the rose? I wasn't going to carry it around Paris. Up ahead was the Lapin Agile, one of Utrillo's bars where he hung out. Its roof would make a good landmark. I threw the rose up over the 8 foot high cemetery rock wall, but it landed on top. The flower was hanging over the edge. This would work. I could spot it when I came back in the morning, get it, and put it on his grave.

The next morning was bright and brisk, cool for September. I was walking on Rue Lepic, back to the cemetery. On the sidewalk, just waking up, was a guy who had been sleeping there for who knows how long. I gave him a couple baguettes, which I had scored from the hostel where I was staying. He gave me a "merci" and a surprised look on his face that said "I didn't even have to ask."

The cemetery gates were wide open, like welcoming arms. I asked the keeper, a different guy this time, where Utrillo was buried. He motioned back to the wall where I had thrown the rose. I found the gravesite, a statue of a woman holding a painter's palette marked the grave. It was right by the wall. Above the grave, on the wall, was the red rose hanging over the edge. My heart beat a little harder, a little faster. I thought about it, but I didn't try to climb the wall and fetch the rose. Where it was - it made do.

Junior High in Smog City

In 1956, my dad got in a little trouble with his employer over dad's union activities as shop steward and was fired. "Jim, you're fired. Here's your check." The job he got fired from was sanding floors.

In Michigan, in those days, almost all the houses were built with tongue-and-groove solid oak floors. As a kid, I went to work with dad a couple times to see how he made us a living. He and his partner did two houses per day, one in the morning and one in the afternoon. You needed skill and strength in order to finish two houses in a day and to make them look perfect.

The sander was a big heavy machine with a belt driven drum that had a coarse piece of sand paper attached to it. You couldn't just fire it up and hit the go button. If you did that, you would make gouges in the wood, ruining the job. You had to start out with the drum turning slowly - nice and easy like - then increase the power little by little.

The sander had a mind of its own. It grabbed and pulled, exerting its will against the man's. The man didn't want to get into fighting the machine. He would get worn down and beaten if he tried that tactic. No, he had to use the machine's strength against itself, guiding it, not horsing it. If you were a master at sanding floors, you could be master at Aikido – the way of harmonious spirit. Same principal, use the strength of the opponent against himself.

In places where the sander couldn't reach, like around the room's baseboard and closets, the worker had to use a smaller handheld sander. This machine was also heavy since it was of industrial grade, not some toy for a do-it-yourselfer. Of course he had to bend over the whole time, a back breaking job.

The final step was sweeping up the saw dust and mopping on a heavy coat of varnish. Dad mopped on the varnish as fast as he could and got out of the house as soon as possible, so he breathed in a minimum of varnish fumes, which caused a headache. Back then no one used a mask.

The house was locked up with the varnish drying overnight. The panel truck was loaded up with the sanders, the broom, the mop, and the cans of varnish. It was time to drive back to the shop in downtown Detroit and go home.

If it was Friday, it was pay day, and dad would stop off at a pizza joint, before there were chain restaurants, and pick up a family size pizza. "Dad's home." In those days, it was hand thrown pie crusts, with button mushrooms, and extremely stringy mozzarella cheese. The shop was owned and operated by Italian-Americans. The pizza was delicious - made with the best of ingredients, not the cheapest - a big treat that all of us enjoyed.

My dad worked several years for Ed Trustkey, his employer. never missing a day's work. Trustkey made a mistake by firing my dad because he lost a good, dependable worker. How many of that kind come through the door looking for a job? My dad was also a skilled carpenter who didn't need Ed Trustkey. He could find another job anywhere, anytime. The firing was a prompt for our family to move out to California.

That summer, dad and mom sold our house, which dad built on Crown Street in Wayne, and packed up the family's possessions. The trailer was stacked high with furniture and cardboard boxes filled with household goods and clothes. A mattress was on top. Mom backed up the two-tone, blue and white, Ford station wagon, and dad hitched up the trailer. My two sisters, Carol and Marcia, got in and away we went to California. I never looked back. "Did you turn off the gas? Okay, let's vamoose out of here."

My folks wanted to move to California because we had been living there once before, and they liked the climate. Right at the end of WWII, my mom and we kids were living in a small house next door to my grandparents on my father's side, who lived in Muscoy. At the time, my dad was a pilot in the war, flying a fighter, the P-39 Airacobra and a two engine Martin Marauder B-26 bomber.

When my dad came home from the Army, I was only about three. I met him outside and ran up to him as he walked up to the house. He was still in his officer's uniform, the bill on his hat smelled like fresh leather. He squatted down, gave me a hug, and said, "I brought you something." He took off the top of a box and showed me the present: a box of Hershey chocolate bars.

Muscoy was hot and dry. When the wind blew, tumbleweeds would scud across the highway, eventually getting hung up on a barbedwire fence. Eucalyptus trees thrived and grew everywhere, lining the dirt roads, giving welcomed shade from the unrelenting hot, punishing sun. There weren't any public pools to go swimming in. You had to come up with your own entertainment as a kid. So maybe you found a stick and hit rocks with it or swung on a rope hanging from a tree. Swinging on a rope was how I broke my arm. When the doctor sawed off the cast with the electric saw - that scared me. I thought he was going to saw off my arm.

Grandpa and grandma lived next door in a house that my grandpa built. The fireplace and a couple exterior walls were built out of rocks, which he found on the vacant one acre lot. In the back, my grandma kept chickens for fresh eggs and Sunday supper. She had a eucalyptus stump in the back yard with white feathers sticking in the top from where she chopped off the heads of chickens before gutting and roasting them. "Find the hatchet for me. It's in the shop." Grandma could do all this without getting a stain on her apron.

Grandma and grandpa had also lived in Michigan, up around Alpena, before they came out to California. They came to California to get out of the Michigan winters, which were really severe. Grandma had gotten pneumonia a couple times in the winter and came pretty close to dying. Dad had said he remembered praying for her with all his might when she was sick because he thought she could die.

Grandpa saw an ad in the paper for a one time job of driving a milk truck out to Arizona from Detroit. After he got to the all year round summer weather of Arizona, he realized that they should move out of the ice and snow, and maybe grandma would have better health.

When he got back to Alpena, they got rid of the farm, packed up and headed out to California. California had the reputation of being warm year round just like Arizona, except maybe not as hot. They went as far west as they could, all the way to the Pacific Ocean. They landed in Laguna Beach in Southern California, which is a very scenic seaside town with a goldilocks climate - not too hot and not too cold. Laguna

Beach is also an artist colony. It would have been perfect for grandma because she was a very talented painter and sculptor. She could have made a good living painting commissioned oil portraits. Laguna Beach would have given her the necessary support with its network of upscale art galleries. But, because Laguna Beach is such an attractive place to live, it is also expensive, even back before WW II.

They came inland about sixty miles and bought a lot in Muscoy, just outside San Bernardino at the foot of the San Bernardino Mountains. Land prices were a lot cheaper there because if someone could afford it, they would probably live where it wasn't so hot, dry, and sandy or where there were other rich people hunkered down under their air conditioners, like in Palm Springs.

Muscoy didn't have an artist community, of course, so grandma didn't pursue the marketing of her talent. That's the way it goes. Being in the right place at the right time can make all the difference as far as financial success for an artist.

It took us about a week to drive out to California in late summer. We never asked "are we there, yet?" The eight cylinder Ford station wagon made the trip without any problem, never breaking a sweat. We crossed Lake Michigan on a ferry then headed west by southwest. We traveled over the high plains, and prairies, across rivers, and over mountains, and finally through the desert. We visited all the major sights coming out: Mount Rushmore, the Badlands, Yellow Stone Park, and places like that. I was most excited by the mountains in the west. The Tetons took my breath away. Dad would read the Burma Shave signs along the way, and we never saw two Burma Shave rhymes that were the same. At night we didn't get a motel; we slept in the station wagon. We put the back seat down and made a bed. I slept on top of the mattress on the trailer in a sleeping bag. The trip was a big adventure for a thirteen year old boy. I was secretly wishing it would never end, and we, as a family, could just keep traveling together, seeing new places every day.

By the time we got to Southern California, the only mishap was to the canvass water bag for the radiator my dad purchased at the beginning of the desert. The bag was hung too low off the front bumper and got a hole worn it in from dragging on the highway. "Look at that! I wasted five dollars!" But we didn't have any tires blow out; I didn't fall off the mattress in the night; we didn't even get sunburned. My Polish grandma, my mother's mother back in Michigan, must have been praying for us.

We found, right away, a house to rent in Highland. Highland is on the western side, on the other side of San Bernardino from Muscoy. San Bernardino is known for a couple things to some people. First, it is where McDonalds opened their first restaurant. Second, San Bernardino, also known as Berdoo, was the spawning grounds for the Hells Angels. A third thing, which hardly anyone knows, is that berdoo is a font that's used on the back of motorcycle gang jackets for lettering.

Some days in the San Bernardino Valley, it was hard to see the six-thousand foot high mountains, which were right in the back yard. In 1956, the smog was thick and toxic, turning the hot sun to an orange through the brown haze. There was nothing done for air quality. Cars burned leaded gasoline, pumping the exhaust unfiltered out into the air for people to breathe and settle in their brain cells and other organs.

Another reason for the thick smog was the topography of the place. Wind from the ocean blew all of Los Angeles' smog east into San Bernardino Valley where it was trapped by mountains on three sides like a big three sided box with no escape. On a rare clear day, though, the place was beautiful with mountains rising up and green orange groves down below on the flats. Red hibiscus and magenta bougainvillea bloomed in front yards, hugging white stucco houses.

School for me was going to start in a couple weeks, entering the seventh grade in a public school, which was the only kind I had attended.

I had enjoyed and gotten a lot out of my grammar school, Cady, back in Michigan. Over my life, probably ninety percent of what I learned and retained from formal education took place in grammar school. I was fortunate in that I got Mr. Johnson as a teacher for the fourth, fifth, and sixth grades. He was a dedicated teacher, giving it his all. He was a real big guy, who had played center for the University of Michigan, the Wolverines football team. He loved football and would play with us kids during recess and after lunch. Actually, it was football practice. Our grammar school had a football team. For the games, when we played other schools, we used helmets and pads because we played tackle, putting our football uniform right over our street clothes. My position was quarter back when we had the ball and linebacker when the other team had the ball. When we practiced, we tackled but didn't wear pads or helmets because we didn't have any. It was tricky in late winter when the snow would turn to slush then freeze into ice. Sometimes the ice would be real gnarly. You could get scuffed and cut up pretty good when you got tackled and went sprawling across the jagged ice. We would play football from September to June, enjoying every second of it. Mr. Johnson enjoyed it as well, maybe more than the rest of us. He just didn't stand on the sidelines during recess; he was right there with us, playing. He would take the snaps and passed the ball, playing with his game face on the whole time. "On three go out for a pass!" In the fifth grade we had a good winning season. In the sixth grade we had a better season, winning all, except losing the last game for the league championship. Looking back on how a couple of the opposing linemen poured through our line, they must have had a couple kids that were held back a grade because they were bigger and stronger than our guys. Those years in grammar school were the only years that I enjoyed organized sports. After the enjoyable years, anytime I had to change out of street clothes and into gym clothes or a uniform, I hated it.

In the fourth grade, when my school mates and I first met Mr. Johnson, we didn't think he was going to be such a great guy - kind of scary. One day in the beginning of the semester, I wasn't in class where I was supposed to be. I was chasing my friend Cal down and through the school hallways. Cal had a picture of a pinup, a woman wearing just a sailor's hat, and I wanted to see more of her. Some people know from little experiences during boyhood that they are gay. Looking back, my experiences were telling me that I was born a flaming heterosexual.

When we got into the classroom, Mr. Johnson was fuming. He picked Calvin up by the head, holding him eye level several feet off the ground with a hand clamped on each side of his head, shaking him back and forth, trying to shout at him but tongue tied in his anger, just spit coming out of his mouth. Mr. Johnson's face was beet red; Cal's face was petrified with fear. I looked on, expecting to hear the snap of Cal's neck, shocked because neither my dad nor any other grownups got physical with me. This was something new. After Mr. Johnson shook the daylights out of Cal, he put him down. Mr. Johnson must have realized he had lost control and had better get hold of himself because he didn't touch me. He just told me to sit down at my desk and warned me not to go gallivanting through the halls. He never did learn the reason why I was chasing Cal. The head shaking incident was the first and last time Mr. Johnson terrorized the class with physical punishment. Sometimes he would be in a bad mood, let it be known that he was a little disappointed with us, and he would act sullen, but he would snap out of it and be his old good natured self the next day. All of us kids loved Mr. Johnson. He really took an interest in us, motivating us to work at learning. I never had a better teacher.

With my past positive experience with grammar school back in Michigan, I was looking forward to the new school year getting started. Little did I know that I was standing by the edge of the rabbit hole about to fall in and down.

The first day, I walked to the junior high by myself. My dad was at work, this time working as a carpenter framing houses in one of the new subdivisions that was springing up everywhere in booming Southern California. My mom was at work, as well, in Riverside, just south of us, in an aircraft factory, sealing rivets. Unfortunately, she worked with some kind of toxic chemicals in the caulk that damaged her lungs and bronchi. The remedy for her lungs was for her to eventually do some other kind of work in the factory that didn't use chemicals. She worked at this factory job for years until she got a job at JC Penny in sales, where she worked well into her seventies.

The walk from our rented house to the school was only about a mile. I walked along a road that once it left the subdivision went right through the orange groves. When the fruit was ripe, it was wonderful to pick an orange and eat it along the way. An orange along the way wasn't stealing, but picking and carrying them home was crossing the line and should be confessed to the parish priest.

The school had a benign welcoming front, convincing all passersby that it was a righteous place. The school had big shade trees out front, planted on a cool green lawn. The main two-story building with administrative offices and classrooms sat out front. It was a clay colored, stucco building that reminded me of a Spanish mission. Behind the two-story mission like building was the main campus with single-story classrooms, gym, shops, and cafeteria. All interconnected with concrete sidewalks, black asphalt areas, and grass lawns out in the PE area. Throngs of unsupervised kids wandered and milled about before first period.

For my first day, I was wearing a clean white shirt freshly ironed by my mother. Going to my first class, an older kid, maybe a ninth grader and about a foot taller, grabbed me by the upper arm, clamping his hand on my shirt sleeve from behind and said, "You're new here, aren't you?"

"Yeah, why?"

"Just wanted to know," he said with a menacing grin and ran off.

I turned on the water fountain to get a drink. Someone had jammed a pencil into the spout so that the water shot up with the intention of hitting the thirsty in the face. I pulled the pencil out and ran the water for a while to clean it.

A teacher walking by said, "Don't play with the fountain. Either get a drink or else leave it alone." She kept on walking to her class.

After getting a drink of water, I noticed that my shirt had a huge indigo ink stain where the kid grabbed me on the arm. Apparently, he had poured ink into his hand and went around grabbing kids, leaving a permanent ink stain. There were trolls before the internet.

Half the boys who were milling about before their first class were grouped in gangs, most had three to five kids in them. The older kids in these gangs cruised around looking for victims to humiliate. One of them would approach a lone kid, a new kid like myself, and intimidate him into shining his shoes with his other gang buddies backing him up.

A gang of five was pounding one brave kid who refused to shine shoes. Blood was running out of his nose and down onto his white t-shirt. The teacher, who had told me to stop playing with the faucet, walked by the beating, as if it wasn't her job to intervene.

The bell rang with its piercing imperative of *get to class or else*. Everyone started running, except for the kid with a bloody nose. He held his nose with one hand and his notebook in the other, staggering to his classroom, crying all the way. He paid the price for standing up to the bullies. It was a lesson to the rest of us – it would cost you a beating to stand up. The teachers offered no protection, and it was law of the jungle - the strong devouring the weak.

My first class was gym, where we were assigned a locker and combination padlock. Our gym teacher, who had a remarkable resemblance to Lee Marvin and even had what sounded like his deep gravelly voice, was named Mr. Piles. We were standing outside on the tarmac on our assigned numbers as Mr. Piles instructed us about what type of gym clothes we were to bring the following morning, giving our mothers only that night to go out and buy red shorts, a white t-shirt, tennis shoes, and an optional jockstrap.

Mr. Piles demonstrated by holding up each piece of the uniform. He put his ever present clip board between his knees and held up a jockstrap, stretching the waist band with both hands out to its max with the business end dangling down. He bellowed, "To the uninitiated, this here is the jockstrap! If you are going to be a serious athlete, I highly recommend the procurement of this item. Every player in the NFL and NBA has one of these in his locker. In Major League Baseball they have a similar piece of equipment called the 'cup.' Here at Highlands, we have no baseball team, as a matter of fact, we will not be playing baseball or softball. We don't have a football team either, but we do have a basketball team. I highly recommend getting a jockstrap. I'm wearing one right now. But, administration in its infinite wisdom has deemed the jockstrap optional. You get a jockstrap, and you will be a certified jock. Any questions?"

One kid raised his hand.

"Yes," Mr. Piles said, consulting his clipboard for a clue to the kid's name, "what is it Martinez?"

"What's it for?"

"Did you hear that, class? Martinez wants to know what's it for. Can any of you tell Martinez what's it for?"

I had no idea what it was for, but it looked nasty. If any of the other seventh graders fresh out of grammar school knew what it was for, they weren't saying. The class was silent.

"No? No one knows. It's to protect your nuts! If you want to have kids someday, the jockstrap will protect your nuts so that you can have kids someday. Without it, you can get ruptured real good. Get ruptured and you don't have kids. Do I make myself clear? Any questions?"

Martinez raised his hand again.

"Yes," said Mr. Piles, consulting his clipboard again, "Martinez, what is it?"

"How do you wear it?" asked Martinez.

"Good question. I'll show you." Mr. Piles set his clipboard on the ground and got into the jockstrap, balancing on one foot at a time until he had the jockstrap over his red gym shorts. He walked back and forth along the whole line of us boys standing in formation, going from end to end, not once, but a couple times until he wound up back in the center where he stopped his promenade and asked, "Any questions?"

None of us had questions. I decided right then that I would never get or wear a jockstrap. Taking a chance on not ever having kids was better than wearing something that looked so weird and nasty.

The kid next to me joked, "Mom, our class has the piles."

"You, there!" said Mr. Piles, pointing at the comedian next to me. "What's so funny?"

"I didn't say anything," said the defiant comedian.

"Get up here!"

The comedian sauntered over to Mr. Piles, who picked up his clipboard. The kid's chubby knees started to shake with fear. Mr. Piles was standing there in his jockstrap over his shorts, holding his clipboard with both hands, taking a few warm up swings. The gym teacher told the boy with shaking knees and red hair, who was standing in front of him, "Turn around, funny boy, face the class, and grab your ankles." The boy turned around. Everyone could see the fear on his face. "Now bend over." The kid bent over.

Mr. Piles smacked the kid across the ass with the clipboard as hard as he could. "Now get back on your number and keep your mouth shut! The rest of you go out to the football field and walk around or something until the bell rings. Remember to bring your gym clothes tomorrow, or else," he said, brandishing his clipboard over his head. Mr. Piles walked off to his office in the locker room, still wearing his jockstrap over his shorts.

I didn't think the other teachers would razz him about his jockstrap style because he might hit one of them in the face with his clipboard.

We seventh graders meandered off to the football field where there were the eighth and ninth graders waiting for us.

"Did that hurt much?" I asked the comedian.

"Nah, not much," he lied. I never heard him murmur another word in that class when Mr. Piles was talking, or when he wasn't talking.

Our class was herded together in a loose circle like wildebeest on the grass field, except all of us were calves, when a gang of five from the eighth grade approached us. The gang half circled us, like a pack of hyenas, looking for one in the herd to cut out and tear apart. They picked this ultra-blonde headed kid who barely spoke English. He was from some country in Eastern Europe, but no one knew exactly where. One of the gang of five picked a fight with the blonde headed kid by calling him a coward and other insults. The bully was going to show off to his gang and the rest of us how bad he was.

The blonde kid was a little bigger with longer arms than the other kid. Both assumed the classic boxing stance, but the blonde headed kid didn't make a fist. The bully threw the first punch, which missed, but the blonde kid countered with a right hand slap across the bully's face, stunning him. The blonde kid hit him again as hard as he could with an open left hand, then a right. Not only was the bully shocked, but also the other four in his gang didn't know what to make of what was going down. The bully was backing up when he stumbled and fell backwards. The blonde kid stood over him, slapping the kid's face first with his right then his left then his right... shouting at the bully in a foreign language that none of us understood. Most of the other kids were cheering him on. Everyone enjoyed watching the bully get his ass kicked in a most humiliating way, getting bitch slapped. The school bell rang, saving the kid on the ground. The blonde headed kid stopped slapping him, and we all went to our next class.

(The next day, another kid, who was bigger than the first, from the same gang picked another fight with the blonde headed kid, who bitch slapped the challenger silly. After that, no one bothered the blonde headed kid, who fought by slapping and spoke a strange language.)

My next class after gym was music. I had liked music in grammar school. Once a week on Fridays, we would have music. Cady had a special teacher for that, a woman, who brought in simple musical instruments like wooden sticks, triangles, tambourines, that sort of thing. We would sing and beat out a rhythm. Also she would play some tune on a portable record player, and we would dance, not only square dancing, but also what she called the fox trot, young boys and girls dancing together.

At Highland Junior High, music class was a different story. We didn't have any musical instruments, not even a couple sticks to bang out a rhythm. We didn't do any singing either. Our music teacher was a young teacher named Miss Grensky. Our classroom didn't have air conditioning, and it was getting hot causing Miss Grensky to sweat.

"Now settle down, class," said Miss Grensky. "I'm your music teacher. Miss Grensky is my name." She wrote her name in large letters on the chalkboard. As she wrote on the board, we could see the big sweat stains under her armpits. "I'm going to play you some music, and I want you to think about it. Think about what type of picture the music is painting. What type of story the music is telling. It's a very famous composition. It is Tchaikovsky's *Overture of 1812*," she said, in a very posh voice. She was going to expose us to culture. It was her duty.

While the overture boomed on, the two boys sitting next to me, who were buddies to each other, entertained themselves by drawing. They drew in ball point pens the same thing on school paper. The subject of their drawings was women's breasts with nails driven through, dripping blood. They didn't do this just for the first day; they did it every day for the semester, four and a half months. They didn't just draw breasts, although that was their favorite subject. They also drew other parts of women's anatomy being mutilated and maimed. While they were drawing, they would compare.

Miss Grensky didn't say anything to them. She may have just been satisfied they were keeping quiet, not disturbing the class; although, she could have been afraid to say anything to them. She never did make eye contact with either after the first day.

After the overture was over, Miss Grensky asked, "Well, class, what was the music saying?"

One kid raised her hand.

Miss Grensky pointed to the girl, "Yes?"

"It sounded like war, like cannons."

"Very good. Yes, war. There was a war in 1812. You're right, war. Anyone else?"

One of the artists next to me raised his hand and said without being asked, "Stabbing. Sounds like stabbing."

"Stabbing?" asked Miss Grensky.

"Yeah, you know, with an ice pick." He mimed stabbing someone.

The bell rang and we went to our next class: math. When I got to my math class, the teacher greeted us with swatting a student's ass with his bat. All of my male teachers hit their students with a modified Louisville Slugger, which were manufactured by the wood shop teacher, who sawed them down into knockoff, narrow cricket bats.

The girls were exempt from getting hit, probably protected by California law. I don't think the teachers would have shown them mercy if they weren't compelled.

The women teachers didn't hit us. Maybe the law said something to the effect that male teachers may paddle male students and didn't spell out that women could jump in as well. Also, it was evident that the law didn't specify what was a paddle and what was a weapon, which could crack a pelvis.

The math class was cut short because the school principal wanted all of us seventh graders in the cafeteria for a sit-down, as they say in mafia movies. We filed into the school cafeteria, where some of us found seats and others stood around the perimeter, leaning up against the wall. The smell of tomato paste was in the air. The chatter of the cafeteria ladies, and the clatter of pots and pans filled the silence of a couple hundred seventh graders gathered together who had a morning taste of terror and who were too scared to talk.

Finally, the principal strolled in followed by his main enforcer the vice principal. The tall, skinny vice principal had a somber face that would have been useful to an inquisitor during the Spanish Inquisition. If the teachers were armed with bats, what did this born-again inquisitor have back in his office? That's what all of us wondered.

The principal was a surprisingly jovial fellow, not much taller than some of us seventh graders. He could have been a professional jockey, but he was too heavy, as round as he was tall. He had an American made, short sleeve, white shirt; blue tie, and glasses with black plastic frames. Even back then there were nerds.

The vice principal made the introduction, speaking into a microphone. "Students, I'm the vice principal, Mr. Napoli. I hope I never have to see any of you in my office. I'm in charge of discipline. I can suspend, or even worse, expel you. You don't want to get expelled. If that happens, you have to go to another school where it's not as good as Highland Junior High.

"To my right is Mr. Winston. He's the school principal. He wants to talk to you since this is your first day of school. Let's give Mr. Winston a big Highland Hornet buzz." He buzzed into the microphone like a pissed off hornet. Our teachers who were in the cafeteria coached us in buzzing. In a few seconds, everyone was buzzing. Mr. Winston let it go on until we were all buzzed out. He took over the mic from his cohort.

"Thank you, Mr. Napoli," said the short, fat man. "Let's give Mr. Napoli a hearty Highland Hornet buzz." He buzzed furiously into the mic, lifting his hand, exhorting us to buzz louder. The whole place buzzed like a hornet's nest. One of the older teachers, a gray haired lady, who was standing along the wall with her English class, passed out and collapsed from the heat and loss of breath from too much buzzing. A couple other teachers came to her aid. A crowd of people was standing around, so I couldn't see what they were doing exactly, but one of the teachers yelled, "Call an ambulance! For God's sake, call an ambulance!" After a while an ambulance showed up and hauled her out of there on a gurney. The ambulance siren faded away as they took her off to the hospital.

After the old teacher was taken away, the principal continued, "This is my favorite time of year, seeing all of these new faces. My, my, my, just look at all these young, fresh faces. I know that all of you will learn a lot in the next three years…"

I thought, "Three years! No! I won't be able to take three years." I offered up to God my first prayer, one of many to follow, to have mercy on me and get me out of this place.

I thought of an angle to get me out; maybe, I could get myself expelled and go to the other school. Highland was good for one thing, prodding me into thinking about survival, figuring the angles to outsmart evil forces that were trying to at least keep me down if not destroy me.

The principal continued, "…Now, as most of you have noticed we have a unique tradition at Highland: hazing. Upper classmen have been hazing for as long as anyone can remember. Some dissatisfied, complaining pansies have complained about hazing and have asked for it to stop. But, that isn't possible, so don't complain about it. You might ask why it can't stop. It's very simple, if you stop to think about it. Because, it wouldn't be fair. It wouldn't be fair to the eighth and ninth graders. You see, when they went through the seventh grade, they were hazed. Now it's their turn to do the hazing. That's the way life is, students. Giving and getting. Getting and giving. Don't worry, when you are eight graders, you'll be the ones doing the hazing. Then when you're ninth graders, you'll be hazing again. So you get one year of being hazed and two years of hazing. Two for one. Who can complain about that? You see now why it wouldn't be fair not to haze?

"Also, I want to tell all of you that the reason you are here is to learn, not to goof around. Be sure to do what your teachers tell you to do. Some of you may have come from grammar schools where the teachers spared the rod and spoiled the child. Well, that's not going to happen here. It's not going to do you any good to go home and cry crocodile tears for your mommy and daddy. How your parents treat you in their homes is their business, but in this school, it's my business and your teachers' business. It's for your own good. When you grow up to be adults with your own kids, you'll look back on your days at Highland and thank us. Without discipline you would run wild, wasting three years, learning nothing, and leaving as dumb as when you first came here.

"If you want to succeed here, and for your sakes I hope you do, do what your teachers tell you. Don't be late for class. Do your homework, and be happy. That's all I've got to say. And, good luck."

Mr. Napoli took back the microphone and said, "Let's give the principal, Mr. Winston, a big Hornet buzz."

We trudged back to our math class, some buzzing along the way, but more creatively by buzzing low then louder, up and down, up and down, until, the math teacher told the buzzers, "Knock it off!"

We got our math books, our first homework assignment, then dismissed to go to lunch.

My mother had given me thirty cents for a cafeteria lunch. She must have liked the idea of not having to make me a lunch before she had to go to work in the morning. The only day she continued to make me a lunch was on Friday. We were Catholics, except my father who was Methodist, so she wanted to make sure I wasn't eating meat on Friday. So on Friday, I would bring the brown paper bag with the tuna fish sandwich stain at the bottom.

Half the kids ate a sensible lunch in the cafeteria. For thirty cents you got something like hamburger helper, mixed vegetables, an apple, and a carton of milk.

The other half, mostly boys who were lucky that Pinocchio was only a fairy tale or else they would have been turned into jackasses, only ate at the snack bar, loading up on sugar. The snack bar eaters usually got the same thing day after day: a strawberry shake, a maple bar, and a bag of Corn Nuts. The more health conscious would get a chili dog, strawberry shake, and maple bar. Combine the sugar with anxiety induced by fear of violence, and you had walking basket cases of nervous wrecks.

Usually the kids with square haircuts, parted on the side with a wave in the front, ate in the cafeteria, and those with ducktails greased up with Brylcreem ate at the snack bar.

The girls, even those with hip, beehive hairdos, mostly ate in the cafeteria, but a few were also getting wound up on the snack bar sugar. They probably went on to a life of alcoholism and drug addiction.

It didn't matter whether you ate in the cafeteria or snack bar, there was no escaping the rock and roll blaring as high as administration could get it cranked up on the PA system. Elvis Presley, the King, was big back then, and that's all they blasted over the outdoor speakers. There was no escaping getting a full dose of the King whether you wanted to hear him or not. "You ain't nothing but a hound dog, crying all the time. You ain't nothing but a hound dog, crying all the time. . ."

After lunch, I was sitting on a concrete wall outside the cafeteria with the PA system blasting Elvis, keeping on guard against roving gangs of hyenas wanting to collect, based upon seniority, their right to humiliate a seventh grader when I overheard a conversation between the school janitor and a school counselor.

"That Billy, you know, the ring leader of that gang of greasy hoods is a real psychopath," the janitor complained to the counselor.

The woman counselor replied, "Yeah, but he's real smart."

The bell rang, and it was time for the next class: science. As long as you got to class on time and didn't make the teacher mad, it was safe. You wouldn't get hit. Despite the violence of the male teachers, the classroom was safer than being out of the class room in areas with the general population where you could get beat up just for some juvenile psychopath's amusement.

Mr. Lee was the science teacher. He was the most vicious. When he hit, he swung for the fences, got his hips into it. There were two schools of thought. Some teachers were all into bat speed and others were power hitters. The ones who were into bat speed had holes drilled into the flat end of the bat to reduce drag from wind resistance.

Others, who were power hitters, didn't have any holes drilled, keeping the weight of their bat to the max. Mr. Lee was one of those who wanted power.

The first day of his class, a couple of the ducktail boys came bopping into class about thirty seconds late. Mr. Lee demonstrated his hitting power. Both boys, who dressed like they were tough little hoods, had to hold back the tears, but they managed.

No one dared talk or even give Mr. Lee eye contact. The two boys who liked to draw sadistic pictures in music class were in this science class. They didn't give Mr. Lee eye contact, much less do any drawing, which was valuable survivor training that they probably used later in life when they were serving time in the State pen for some heinous crime, such as mayhem or murder.

Although it was perfectly quiet in Mr. Lee's class, it was difficult hearing what he was saying because he spoke so low, almost whispering, when he taught. His whispering wasn't soothing. It was a little menacing. Many actors in Hollywood have used this technique to play the part of a serial killer. Despite not being able to hear what he was saying, no one dared to ask him to talk louder. Also, you couldn't sit closer, because seats were assigned by alphabetical order. This was the standard operating procedure, which was pretty smart, because it separated the trouble makers who were stronger when they were together. If the women teachers weren't going to use violence to have power over the kids, they needed techniques like this one of divide and conquer to gain control.

Because we were assigned seats in alphabetical order, I had a student by the name of Hill who sat behind me in a few of my classes, including science. Hill never said a word, never. He also had green teeth. They weren't green from eating something that was green, like spinach. They were green from just never brushing his teeth.

After school, I thought it was going to be dangerous walking home, but thankfully it was safe. I saw no one else walking on the road through the orange groves. I supposed the gangster hyenas took the bus. By the late afternoon, the temperature was over a hundred, but the heat was less discomforting than the psychological stress of being at school.

It was such a welcomed relief waking up on Saturday morning - no school. The only school I had to go to was catechism, Catholic Sunday school, except it was on Saturday morning. My mom took my sister Marcia and I to the church for religious education. While we were getting our instruction, mom was doing the weekly grocery shopping.

The church we attended was St. Adelaide, the patron saint of abuse victims. The parish was so new that the church hadn't been built yet. Mass was held in the priest's home, which was an old, wooden, two story house painted white, surrounded by an orange grove on Baseline Avenue. We had our catechism class in the living room that also served as the sanctuary for Sunday mass. It was hot in there, even in the morning, with only a swamp cooler. For some reason, maybe it was to try and keep the house cooler by pulling down the shades and closing the drapes, the inside was dark with low lighting and dark furniture.

Some of the furniture was exotic hand carved chairs and tables made in Africa, where Father McNelis had served before being assigned as pastor of this new parish. Father was a Jesuit, who wore the long black cassock with a dozen buttons down the front. He was originally from Ireland and kept his brogue, thankfully. It was a pleasure listening to him talk, which sounded more like someone singing or reciting poetry, even when he was only talking about everyday things, like how hot the weather was.

Father was a kind man, so there was no dread the night before about having to go to catechism. That wasn't the way it was back in Michigan. There, nuns taught catechism after Sunday mass. The strict women in their black and white habits kept an eye on us while we were in church, making sure we were behaving. I would take out my rosary and mumble my lips like I was praying and pass the beads through my fingers. This tactic kept the nuns off my case, and they left me alone. God was probably thinking, good one, son, I would do the same thing.

On Saturday night the anxiety of having to go to catechism and face the women in black and white would ratchet up. Every week they would assign something for us to remember: the essential Catholic prayers, Ten Commandments, that sort of thing. We better have them memorized or else suffer the wrath of the number one sister in charge. Back in the fifties, there wasn't a shortage of nuns, so we always had at least three in the classroom. The oldest one, the mean one, was in charge. She was on the petite side and wrinkled up with age. She didn't tolerate any goofing around and wouldn't hesitate to smack the back of a kid's knuckles with a ruler when it came to snickering about "thou shall not commit adultery." Rapping of the knuckles wasn't so bad. The worse part was that she marched in like she was taking away the innocent in trucks to their doom, never smiled, and never cracked a joke. We never gave an excuse for not being prepared, not having memorized the Our Father or the Hail Mary because she didn't want to hear any excuses. We never tested her to see if she had more up her big sleeve besides the ruler treatment. She won; we submitted.

I have to admit, she got results. We learned what we were supposed to learn, and I have never forgotten it. The learning came at the high price of anxiety, not hers of course. Saturday night, cramming to memorize whatever I was supposed to memorize, filled me with anxiety. After my experience with memorizing as a way to learn, I avoided it at all costs. Don't ask me what the words are to the National Anthem.

With his Irish charm and good sense of humor, Father McNelis, didn't scare me or make me anxious. He didn't make us memorize anything. He taught the lessons to us, about six kids in the class. Instead of teaching doctrine, he taught about Jesus by telling us the gospels in the New Testament, starting in the beginning and going through to the resurrection. He talked about Jesus as if he were walking the face of the earth, rather than being long gone. The lessons were interesting, and I enjoyed being there. They also came in useful for giving me guidelines about how to live and what to expect of God. I went on to expect God to heal the sick and someday raise the dead, a God of miracles. He was certainly capable of getting me out of Highland Junior High.

On Sunday morning, there were about ten families, or so, attending worship. At that time, the mass was in Latin, and women had their heads covered with a scarf or a fancy handkerchief. Besides starting the new parish, which included the construction of a church, Father also taught algebra at the Catholic high school on Sterling Avenue called St. Aquinas as if he didn't have enough work to do. I wanted to go to this school, thought it would be a good place to learn if Father was teaching there. I mentioned this desire to my folks one time, but the idea of spending money at a private school when I could go to a free public school was out of the question. I never mentioned it again after that. I didn't know if they could afford it or not. Even if they could afford it, dad would have been opposed to it on the grounds that I would run the risk of getting spoiled and turned into a snob from rubbing elbows with those who thought public school wasn't good enough for them.

Construction of the new church began around October. On Saturdays, my dad, even though he wasn't Catholic and went to a Methodist church, volunteered to help build it. Since my dad was a master carpenter able to build a house from beginning to end on his own, he was a valuable volunteer. The building went up fast, completed by Christmas, and was a little jewel, with an open vaulted ceiling made of red cedar and imported Italian stained glass windows. I spent a lot of time looking in awe at the windows. Rather than just being a mosaic of colored glass, the details, especially in the faces of the figures were painted by an artist of outstanding skill, something rare. Once this beautiful church was built, attendance started to pick up and was always full on Sundays. During high mass with the burning incense and the soloist singing Ave Maria, it was a beautiful sanctuary from the outside world with its Highland Junior High.

Once in a while, Father's Mexican housekeeper, an old lady, made and sold chicken tamales. She made them the old fashioned way of cooking them in the corn husk and leaving in parts that normally you don't want to eat, like the esophagus. She always dressed in black and was a mysterious woman, speaking in a secret language: Spanish with a Mexican accent.

About six years later, when I had escaped from the area by joining the Army, Father McNelis was transferred to another parish out in the desert. With a new priest as pastor, one of the parishioners brought in her own candles and accidentally burned down the church, destroying everything including the beautiful stained glass windows. Father was still alive when this happened and must have been shocked when he heard the news.

A new, bigger church was built on the ashes. A cross made out of charred cedar beams was constructed and put up in the garden that had one remaining orange tree from the original orchard, which had given way to more houses. The parish grew from the original ten families to over nineteen hundred families. Probably the parish priest didn't teach catechism, too busy for that. The parish got bigger, but we had the best years when Father taught us catechism in the old house and sun shined through stained glass windows painted with images of Jesus and the saints.

God answered my prayers for getting me out of Highland Junior High by the next semester. My folks bought a new house in a new subdivision out in the Del Rosa neighborhood, putting me in another school district. I started in the spring semester and figured it had to be better. It was. None of the teachers, except the gym teachers, had bats or hit the kids. In the two and a half years that I was there, I was hit only once by a gym teacher with a bat. He was a big monster named "Tiny." My crime was running in the locker room, which I was doing so that I wouldn't get beat up by another kid. At the time, I thought it was worse to admit to running from a fight than it was to get hit once by "Tiny." The kid chasing me, didn't get hit, which was another underlining of my growing mistrust of authority figures like "Tiny." Learning to mistrust authority proved to be a valuable survival skill later in life.

The new school was a big improvement by being less of a fear factory. It was a relief to know that if I was a few seconds late for class, I wouldn't be hit. Hazing wasn't institutionalized. Although there were packs of hyenas, they seemed to be fewer. Maybe, because the male teachers were less violent, the students were less violent. Over the two and a half years I was there, I got in a few fights out of self-defense, but it was no big deal.

Defending myself didn't get much support back home. My dad had told me not to fight way back in Michigan because he was going through his Bertrand Russell phase at the time. Easy for my dad to preach pacifism as the way, but he wasn't having to go to public school at the time. It couldn't have been much better for him in his school days since he quit high school and ran away from home on the farm for the big city lights of Detroit. If school was a good place to be, why did he quit when he was sixteen? When I saw Bertrand Russell's picture on one of the books my dad was reading, the philosopher was holding a pipe. I wondered, "If Bertrand Russell is so wise, why is he smoking a pipe?" My mistrust of authority was for all sorts of authority. I was an equal opportunity skeptic.

Although the culture of violence weren't as bad at the new school, the curriculum and teaching wasn't any better. None of the teachers sparked any enthusiasm for any of the subjects.

The most memorable teacher was the shop teacher, Mr. Whittle, because I took four classes from him. I took so many classes, not because he was a gifted teacher, but he was the only shop teacher at the school.

Mr. Whittle was a nondescript person. He wasn't tall or short, wasn't fat or skinny, wasn't old or young. He didn't talk much, so we never got to know him very well. He always wore a brown shop coat, like he was ready to work, but after the first day he never touched a tool. The most outstanding thing about Mr. Whittle was the heavy tobacco stains on his fingers, which went with his brown shop coat. He spent most of his time in his office, smoking and reading magazines, like *Popular Mechanics*. The shop coat he wore wasn't just for show; it came in handy by keeping cigarette ash from falling on his street clothes and burning small holes.

Mr. Whittle was a master at working the system. He did a minimum of work, an amount so small that you would think it would be impossible to do so little and still keep his job. He taught drafting, wood shop, and metal shop. It was mandatory to take an elective. If you were a boy student, your path would eventually cross Mr. Whittle's , who would school you in how to do so little over such a long period of time.

Just about every kid, tens of millions, in the public school system in the 50's took drafting. The country was obsessed with it; as if we were all going to be sitting at our drawing boards and T-squares at home, drawing up blue prints and working drawings of carburetors or sitting on high stools in the drafting department at Boeing.

The only day Mr. Whittle gave instruction was on the first day. After taking attendance, he said, "Gather 'round. I want to show you somethin'." We all gathered around, looking over one another's shoulders to see what he was doing. "You put your piece of paper like so on the T-square, lining up the edge…" Then he would proceed to do a simple drawing out of the workbook. "You see, it's just a matter of copying the drawing."

The next day, when the class would show up for drafting, Mr. Whittle would take attendance then go into his office for a smoke, which showed us that there was some truth to the saying "ninety percent of it is just showing up."

In the beginning of the semester, a kid might ask, naively expecting help, "Mr. Whittle how do you..."

"I showed you. Just copy your work book," was Mr. Whittle's stock answer for all questions. This also was a lesson; in that, we learned that stock answers took all the effort out of thinking and communicating and would suffice.

After a few days, the kids would learn that it was useless to ask anything and would just leave Mr. Whittle in peace, in his office, to smoke his cigarettes.

Drafting wasn't too bad when we used a pencil, which was the first semester. I could erase mistakes and go on, but the second semester when we had to use india ink, it was frustrating. There wasn't anything to erase a mistake like a glob of ink or drawing past the end point. Mr. Whittle wouldn't accept any drawings in ink with any glitches, which meant that the drawing had to be started over from scratch once a glitch was made. I never completed a single ink drawing, but started a ton of them. Mr. Whittle might have been amused by all the frustration, but I couldn't tell because he never smiled, just had a blank expression on his face all the time.

After drafting one and two, the next semester I took metal shop. Mr. Whittle's modus operandi was the same in metal shop as it was in drafting. After taking roll, he demonstrated what we were to make. We had one project for the semester, make a barbeque fork and spatula set.

While he was taking roll, he had a couple steel rods with their ends heating up in the forge.

"Watch out! This thing is hot!" Mr. Whittle exclaimed, surprising all of us with the energy he put into his warning. He took one of the rods, which was glowing cherry red out of the roaring forge, and swung it in an arc, nearly branding a couple kids who leaned back just in the nick of time. He walked it over to the anvil and commenced beating the red end with a hammer. He got the second rod out and hammered the end of that one just like the first.

"Watch out!" he said again. With all the exclamations, Mr. Whittle was throwing around, we knew that we were dealing with some dangerous stuff. I was thinking that when Mr. Whittle went back to his office and turned us loose, there was going to be some serious injuries when these idiots started playing grab ass with red hot metal.

After about forty five minutes of hacksawing, drilling, riveting, filing, reheating and shaping, Mr. Whittle had fashioned a set of barbeque tools - fork and spatula with no handles. He was fast. No telling how many of these he had made over his career.

Mr. Whittle held up his work and said, "The last thing you'll have to do is sand off the black and polish them. Each of you have been given some of this Emory cloth. Don't lose it. You're only going to get one piece. A big part of your grade will be based upon how shiny you can make them."

I thought this was awesome, that we were going to be making things out of metal, heating it up and hammering it out, just like in the westerns with scenes in the black smith shop. The barbeque set was the beginning project with others to make after finishing this one. This was going to be interesting.

The next day we got busy, and I was right. Two kids were sword fighting with their cherry red steel rods, and one of the kids got branded on the arm. Mr. Whittle came out of his office. "How did this happen?" he demanded, cigarette smoke leaking out of his nostrils.

"It was an accident," said the one who did the branding.

"Is that right?" Mr. Whittle asked the injured trooper.

The kid with the two inch, third degree burn nodded his head "yes."

"Go down to the school nurse, and have her take a look at it."

"Where is she?" asked the burned victim.

"She's got an office down in administration. You know, where the principal has his office. She's down there. You can find it. Better get going."

The kid started walking to where he was directed to go. When he got to the shop door, Mr. Whittle said, "Don't forget your books, you might not be coming back."

The kid turned around, got his books, and slumped off to the nurse's office. Mr. Whittle walked back to his office, shaking his head, muttering to himself. We went back to working on our projects. The happy sound of a hammer hitting soft metal on an anvil filled the shop.

It took another three days to make the barbeque set. For the rest of the semester, over four months, we polished our forks and spatulas with the little piece of Emory cloth. The biggest take away lesson was how tough Emory cloth is. Sure it got worn down to the smoothness of silk, but it never tore.

Although the fork and spatula didn't have handles, I had big dreams of making handles for them out of deer antlers when my dad shot a buck during the next deer season. In the meantime, and also to hedge my speculation about dad supplying the antlers, I signed up for wood shop for the next semester.

Mr. Whittle on the first day showed us how to build our projects, a bread board out of a single pine board and a TV serving tray out of quarter inch plywood and a couple pieces of mahogany screwed onto the sides for handles. After demonstrating how to use the power table saw with a short safety training session "don't cut off your fingers," Mr. Whittle held up a piece of sandpaper and said, "You will be issued three pieces of sandpaper: coarse, medium, and fine. Don't lose them because you aren't getting anymore."

I was expecting at least one kid to saw off the end of a finger or two, but it didn't happen. Word had gotten out about the branding in metal shop during the prior semester, and kids weren't all that eager to fool around with anything that could maim them. Also you couldn't have a sword fight with table saws. By this time, the branding accident had gotten spun into an urban legend. The kid didn't get burned on the arm, but the red hot poker had been stabbed into his eye, blinding him for life.

We were done with sawing and screwing our bread boards and TV trays into shape by the beginning of the second week. The remaining four months were spent sanding the projects with the bulk of the time spent on the bread board because it was three times thicker than the TV tray. If all that sanding was done only on the TV tray, it would have had a big hole sanded right in the center. Maybe that hole could be used as a cup or glass holder, but it wasn't part of the project, so we never went there. The takeaway lesson was that sandpaper is not as tough as Emory cloth. We had already learned that busy work could pass for work way back in drafting, not a new takeaway.

In the seventh grade, I had entertained the idea of being an architect when I grew up, but the experience with drafting - mostly the frustration with making glitches and having to start all over - threw enough water on that spark of interest to permanently extinguish that ambition. The school in general, just not shop, was good at throwing water on dreams and ambitions.

If I would have had some desire to be a blacksmith, welder, sheet metal worker, metal sculptor, cabinet maker, wood worker, or carpenter that would have been killed by eight months of boredom from polishing and sanding. Besides, I saw how hard my dad worked sanding floors and got fired for his efforts, so going into the trades was never on my list of things to do. The time in Mr. Whittle's classes fulfilled the formal education system's requirement for so many hours of electives to be taken. The system didn't require that we learn anything.

We drafting and shop students may not have learned much about woodworking and other shop skills, but we learned a valuable life skill from Mr. Whittle's example and from those years spent in junior high. We learned that there was a place in the world for those of us who wanted to give the least if we had to give anything. It was okay to be a slacker and not care. We wouldn't starve. We just had to find our place, not our place in the sun, but our place in some back office in some large corporation or government bureaucracy where we could smoke cigarettes and look at magazines or, better yet, surf the web all day. Somewhere out there in the great corporate landscape, maybe at Google, is a man with green teeth, surfing the web, getting ready to retire.

A Sure Thing

A little, ordinary, brown sparrow was perched on a tree branch outside the hospital window. I watched it turn its head from side to side, like a jaywalker checking for traffic before crossing the street. Then it took off and flew away. I turned my attention to the plastic bag of blood, my blood. It wasn't going in, it was going out. I dozed off.

A nurse was shaking my shoulder and telling me, "Wake up! Wake up!"

"O.k., I'm awake. All done?"

"Just have to get you unplugged. Sit up, then stand up slowly. You might be a little light headed."

I got up and collected the $10 gift certificate for the local Burger King. It was the hospital's way of showing how much they appreciated the blood donation; although, there was no telling how much they were going to charge a patient for it. I wasn't complaining. I hadn't had a square meal, unless you count cigarettes and beer, for a few days. The food would help me survive another day in this hell hole called the L.A. basin. I had been down here for about six months going to training at a hospital to become an x-ray technician. They paid a stipend, which was enough for my room at the local flop house and a few crusts of bread, but better not expect jam and butter. My addictions were polishing off my meager savings. I was at the end of my rope, but it wasn't breaking because I was so skinny. I was hanging on.

There were six of us in the class. We had class instruction for two hours a day and worked in the x-ray department the other six. I could handle the class work, the tests and the theory. But when it actually came down to taking good x-rays, I was pretty lousy at it. About half the time I would have to take the x-ray over again. It was either over or under exposed or missing parts of the lungs or whatever. This particular morning started out by giving lower GI's. I was giving this one old geezer a barium enema when he exploded the stuff out of his anus with about 200 pounds of air pressure. It sounded like a tire blowing on the freeway, and he got me good. Poop splattered all over my white polyester smock. I hate polyester, especially with poop on it.

I got on my bicycle and pedaled off to Burger King. No light headed feeling. If I could survive my hangovers, I could survive giving a pint of blood. If I had it, I would give a pint every day just for the $10. I was locking up my bike outside Burger King to a light pole when this portly elderly gentleman in a three piece black, pin striped suit said in an English accent, "Excuse me, sir, would you like to see my pictures?"

My lock clicked shut, and I said, "You got the wrong fella. I don't have any money."

He gave me a look that said, "Is that all you got? 'Don't have any money.' What are you doing going into Burger King if you don't have any money?" But he didn't say any of that. He said in the mumble of the English aristocracy, "Sir, I'm Lord Hampton, related to the Queen Mother. She's my second cousin. Are you a patron of the arts, sir?"

I was dumbfounded. Sometimes the truth is the last thing that should be spoken.

"Just have a look." He pulled out of his jacket pocket a couple drawings he had done on green lined steno paper with a dull pencil. One picture was of several stick figure horses with stick figure jockeys riding them, about as good as some of my x-rays - lousy. The other was a self-portrait done with just a few lines – actually brilliant. I liked it. I looked at his face. He was waiting for a comment. I looked at the self-portrait again. The few lines told a story of a man who had been down in his luck for a very long time.

I told him, "This self-portrait is quite good. Actually it's better than good. It's brilliant."

His face beamed with pride. "You can have it for a fiver."

Now what was I supposed to do. I just told him how good his drawing was, now I'm going to tell him I don't want to buy it. I didn't want to buy it. What was I going to do with a picture? What I needed was a bus ticket out of town. But he had me. I wasn't going to kick a man when he was down. I knew there was only two bucks in my wallet.

I opened my wallet and held out the two bucks. "This is all I got, sorry. Like I said, you got the wrong fella."

He reached out and took the two bucks and took back his stick drawing of the horses.

I looked at the self-portrait again and said, "This is art. I've got an eye for this sort of thing. I'll have to frame this and hang it in a special place," and I meant it.

He must have sensed that I meant it, because now he changed the relationship from street hustler versus mark to one of friendship. Since I was now his friend, he was going to do me a favor and give me some valuable information. Not the meaning of life, or what I was supposed to do with my life, but the name of the winning horse in the sixth race at Hollywood Park.

"You play the gee-gees?" he asked.

"Once in a while," I lied. Actually I was down at the track about twice a week. Besides being lousy at taking x-rays, I was also lousy at picking horses. My thing, the thing I was lucky at was pro football. The money I made on the NFL went for the hay-burners at the track. The track was a handy temptation, about a half mile from my flophouse.

"Well, my boy, play the third horse in the sixth race at Hollywood Park tonight."

"Has it got a name?"

Again, he could tell that I was sincere, not humoring him. "Rowdy Yankee."

"I know this horse. I've seen him run."

"Pace, my boy, pace. He's a pacer, not a thoroughbred."

"Yes, of course. I know. He's a very good horse." Pacers run or pace, whatever, once a week. They aren't like thoroughbreds that run their guts out, then have a long time to recupe'. I saw him win twice in a row and win easily with style, head held high going across the finish line, way out in front of the other horses. I was going to bet on him next go round. Only one catch, I don't think the teller at the betting window would take a Burger King gift certificate. Not a dime in my pocket. "You think it's a sure thing?"

He mumbled, "I would bet my estate on it."

It looked to me that the two bucks he made off me was his estate, so he probably wasn't exaggerating.

"Thanks for the tip," I said. I thought, maybe this is an omen. Maybe I can hock my bike or something and make a bet.

"You're quite welcome."

"I got a ten dollar gift certificate for giving some blood today. Do you want a hamburger or something?" I gestured towards the entrance door.

"Oh no, my dear boy, but thank you. The Queen Mother has invited me to dine with her and the Prince. But thank you anyway. Toodaloo." Lord Hampton, I'm sure he was Lord Hampton in his own mind, going away mumbled, "Third horse, sixth race, third horse, sixth race."

I thought to myself, "If he says it one more time, I'm betting it."

He looked back over his shoulder at me, looked me in the eye and said very slowly, "Third horse, sixth race."

I got some food in Burger King, felt better, felt lucky. I thought of a plan for getting some cash. I pedaled back to my flophouse, changed out of my whites into a pair of Levis and a sweater, grabbed my check book with a balance of five dollars and headed for the check cashing place before they closed.

I had been in this check cashing place before, cashing my stipend checks, and any personal checks when I had some savings left. They knew me and never had a problem with the paper I brought in.

I wrote a bad check for a hundred bucks. All I had to do was get cash in my account tomorrow and everything would be all right. Rowdy Yankee would just have to do again what he had been doing and win. The girl behind two inch bullet proof glass gave me five twenties and joked that she would trust anyone who wore a sweater like the one I had on.

I told her, "Right." We both laughed a little.

Hollywood Park was lit up in a hopeful halo of light. This was church, and I was about to get saved. I got there by the third race. The racing program had Rowdy Yankee as the fourth horse in the sixth race. So what if the old man had the wrong number, three instead of four, just a simple mistake. The number three horse was Jim Dandy. I remembered it coming in behind Rowdy Yankee. The racing program confirmed this. It had always finished second to my horse, the closest he came was six lengths behind. No contest. I placed my bet on Rowdy Yankee.

I bet the third, fourth, and fifth race in my head. I was there that night to make some money so I could get out of town and back home. I wasn't there to screw around. I was there just for this sure thing. The funny thing is that two out of three horses I picked as winners actually won. I was feeling good but extremely high on adrenalin when the horses for the sixth race came out on the track. There was Rowdy Yankee, head held high, lifting his legs with style, doing a victory dance before he had even run. They warmed up, then got behind the pace car. At the start line, the pace car took off and they were away. Rowdy Yankee found a position along the rail in the number three slot by the first quarter. By the half mile pole, he was second, right behind Jim Dandy the number three horse. No big deal. This was his style. In the last quarter he made his move to pass Jim Dandy. I squeezed the life out of my winning ticket. Jim Dandy's rider put the whip to his horse. Rowdy Yankee caught him and they were neck and neck. Rowdy Yankee's driver never gave him the whip and looked like he was holding him back. Jim Dandy won by a full length. My adrenalin crashed. I had that horrible sinking feeling of doom. I realized the third horse actually won in the sixth race.

I needed a drink and some quiet time to think of my next move. I wound up on the barstool of the dive bar, El Sombrero, across the street from my flophouse. I talked the owner, Rosie, into giving me the Buds on my tab. About two in the morning, closing time, I was pretty well tanked. My only idea that I could come up with was to hock my watch and bike. Maybe I could get a hundred out of both of them to cover the bad check, but probably not. Whatever I could get for them was going on Sunday's game. The alcohol assured me that my luck hadn't run out, that I was still the smartest football gambler who ever lived. I walked out of the bar and across the street to my place. I had to be at the hospital for work in five hours and needed some sleep.

"Darn it," I said to myself. The front door to the flophouse was locked and I didn't have a key. Everything was dark. No use banging on the door. The manager was a grouch and wouldn't bother opening it. My room was on the second floor, overlooking the alley. I went around the back, climbed up the drain pipe, opened the window and crawled in. I turned on the light. I noticed the drawing, the self-portrait of the old man, lying on the nightstand. I took it and stuck it in the corner of a framed Cezanne print of the mountain he had painted all the time. The Cezanne print was on the opposite wall of my bed. I thought, "There, I did it. It's framed and in a special place." I looked at the drawing, a portrait of long suffering. Cezanne's art didn't move me, but the old man's did.

I got undressed, turned off the light, set my alarm and got under the covers. I thought about the sparrow I had seen outside the window earlier. I thought about what Jesus said about how important the life of even a sparrow was to God. I thought about that for a while, then turned off my alarm. I could get a good night's sleep, because I was quitting my lousy job in the morning.

Sarge

A woman's hand with chunky fingers reached into her Levi's pocket and pulled out a crumpled dollar bill, feeding the jukebox, taking a couple tries to get it right. The juke reached out with its digital connections and played a Patsy Cline oldie "Crazy." The jukebox, like the aurora borealis, sent out red, yellow, and green light into the darkness of the beer bar called the Broken Promise. Patsy Cline sent out her song like a woman in love with the wrong man.

Sarge, the woman playing the tune, was in her midlife, maybe ten years past it, wearing a red sweat shirt with orange lettering that read *"Semper Fi."* Her salt and pepper hair was fashioned in a man's style with a part and the sides combed back with a big wave in front cresting and breaking. She played on the woman's football team when she was younger and was a tough nose guard with her bull dog build. When she retired from the Marine Corps, her ambition was to let the hair on her chin grow out into a goatee. She accomplished that ambition. She wouldn't be entering the Miss Sacramento Beauty Pageant any time soon.

Sarge stood with her pool cue in hand, mesmerized by the juke box, standing in its colored lights. The twelve beers she had that night, putting in her shift as a steady customer, helped the juke cast its spell.

"Your shot," Vicky told Sarge, after missing a shot on the pool table. Vicky had a build that a brick house would be proud of. Her legs in her Levis went from the heels of her motorcycle boots up to her "Runaways MC" jacket. She had her long hair dyed black, very common for her millennial generation. Sarge, deep in a trance, didn't hear her, so Vicky hollered again, "Sarge! Hey Sarge!" Sarge snapped out of her pause mode and turned to Vicky who said, "Your shot."

Sarge took her shot, missed the corner pocket with the 5 ball, which rattled in and out. "Damn," she cursed under her breath.

"Ah, too bad," Vicky said, feigning sympathy.

"Sure, Vicky. Sure."

Vicky put the cue behind her arched back, propped her left hip on the pool table, and sunk the 2 ball. She gangsta strolled over to the other side of the table and sunk the 8.

Sarge wasn't that much of a pool player, but she was an expert drinker. Holding up her empty Heineken bottle she hollered over to the bartender, Laura, "How about another one and one for Vicky, too. Would ya'?"

Laura was the owner of the Broken Promise. Her parents came over from Sudan when Clinton was in the White House. She looked like she belonged on the cover of *Vogue*, not tending a dive, beer bar in Sacramento. Laura was tall and graceful, the color of copper, and she had gray eyes. She wore her hair in dreads, and if you wanted to know anything about reggae, ask her. She thought the influence of hip hop had put a commercial dagger through the heart beat of reggae. She would have had just reggae, old school, on the juke, but she knew her customers. American female singers is what they wanted to hear, so that's what she had on the juke.

"No way, I'm closing. It's two o'clock already. You got to get out of here. Cut me a break," Laura admonished Sarge.

"Okay, okay. No problem."

Sarge and Vicky put up their cues in the wall rack and took their seats at the bar. Vicky pulled up a stool next to Terry, another twenty something on the butch side, who also wore a Runaways jacket. Vicky gave Terry a big juicy French kiss with one eye on Sarge, rubbing it in that she had someone and Sarge didn't.

Patsy Cline wailed on about how crazy she was for loving some guy, and Sarge remarked, "That's one crazy sister. Give these two love birds a beer."

"I'm closing! Didn't you hear me? Damn!" Laura continued counting money from the till.

"Alright, alright. Just get me one to go, but open it, would ya'? I don't want to hunt for an opener."

Laura made a note of her cash count, opened the cooler, found a green glass bottle of Heineken, and put it on the bar in front of Sarge.

"Put it on my tab, would ya', sweetie?"

"Forget it. It's on me." Laura went back to her accounting, rolled up the cash register tape, and marked it with the date.

Terry said to Vicky, "Let's get out of here. The last one back has to clean out the litter box in the morning."

Both Terry and Vicky dashed out the bar into the stripmall's parking lot, with rain pouring down, got on their Harleys, and rumbled off down Stockton Blvd. in South Sacramento.

"Wish I had some of that young stuff," Sarge said to Laura, taking a swig of beer.

"Which one, Vicky or Terri?"

"Vicky, of course. What a bod'. Can't see me and Terri. It would be like two porcupines lying in bed."

"She's kind of mean, don't you think?"

"I was in the Marines for thirty-five years. I think I could handle a little bitchiness."

"I'm sure you got your share in your day."

"You got that right."

"Where was it the best?"

"Philippines, no doubt about it. Fell in love so many times. ..." Sarge had a look on her face that said she was remembering some very good times.

"Did you have to pay for it?"

"My best girl had a couple kids, so I didn't mind giving her money. Felt like I was doing something good. You know, keeping the kids fed and clothed. Even a gal like me has a lot of mother in her. Amazing isn't it? Don't you think it's amazing?" Sarge slurred.

"Yeah, simply amazing. You're too faced to drive. I'll call a cab."

"That's sweet of you, but don't worry about it. I'll crash in my camper tonight."

"Again?"

"That's why I got the thing."

"You ever go camping in it?"

"Camping? Like in the woods or something? Nah, I hate camping."

"Just camping in parking lots, out in front of bars, right? Drink up. I got to get out of here and catch me some z's."

Sarge guzzled the remaining beer, and both women left the bar. Laura got in her Fiat and drove away to be back the following morning for another long day.

Sarge walked over to her brown Ford F-150 pickup with a camper on the back, which looked like a giant snail. Before climbing up and in for the night, she dropped her Levis, squatted down and took a leak. She looked at the heavy rain hitting the puddles reflecting the strip mall lights. She thought, how beautiful! Never saw it like this before. After her bladder was empty, she was ready to settle down.

Inside the camper, she was cozy in her sleeping bag, which hadn't been to the cleaners for a few years. She lied on her side, listened to the rain pelt the camper's roof. She started to regurgitate the beer and the Big Daddy sausage that was her supper. She wasn't going to throw up, she was too much of a trooper for that, but she couldn't keep the beer, the sausage, and the stomach acid from bubbling up and into her esophagus. "Oh, crap!" she complained.

She got out of her rack, opened the camper door, and spat out the nasty stomach contents that had worked their way up to her throat and into her mouth. She turned on the light and tried to find something to drink to wash out her mouth, which tasted like Drano. She couldn't find anything in the fridge, and the water tank was empty. She got on her Nikes and climbed down the metal ladder hanging on the bumper to the cold outside. She scooped up a couple handfuls of water from a puddle and washed out her mouth. She scooped up another handful and drank the cold water, soothing her burning throat. "Ah, that's better. Damn sausage."

She climbed back up into her camper, turned off the light, kicked off her shoes, and got back into her sleeping bag. She lied there, waited to see if anymore was going to come up. No. She could safely go to sleep now and not worry about choking on her own vomit, but couldn't go to sleep until she had said her prayers. She snored the night away like a bear in her den, hibernating away the long winter, dreaming about a stream filled with salmon.

The next morning, the rain had stopped, and a few cars were in the stripmall's parking lot. Laura opened the door to her establishment, turned off the alarm, turned on the lights, and dropped the morning paper on the bar just the way she had done for over a thousand times, with the grace and moves of a ballet princess.

Sarge eventually made her way into the bar, and Laura, reading the paper, greeted her with, "Good morning, sunshine."

Sarge headed directly to the restroom, greeted Laura on the way with, "What's the word?"

"Thunderbird," Laura replied, not looking up from her paper.

"Who drinks it the most?" Sarge kept walking to the restroom.

"Colored folks," Laura answered her, like she had done for over a thousand times on a thousand mornings.

Having taken care of her morning business in the women's toilet - the place doesn't have a men's - Sarge was ready for another day, hunkered down on a barstool by Laura. "Give me a beer and a tomato juice. Put it on my tab, will you?"

"Still got a buzz on, eh?"

"Buzz? How about a roaring chain saw. I'm getting too geriatric for this crap." Sarge, with blood shot eyes and a face like a bulldog, looked at Laura.

"Might as well enjoy it before they shuttle you off to some old veteran's home."

"Enjoy it. Good one! How come they never show the merry partygoer with a really bad hangover on those beer commercials or someone with their head in the toilet, throwing up?" Sarge always complained the morning after.

"A little of the hair of the dog that bit you will make a new woman out of you." Laura pulled a Heineken out of the cooler.

"Ah, ah, ah, make it a Millers. I don't think that Dutch stuff is settling too good on my stomach, kind of sour."

Laura put back the Heineken and got her a bottle of Miller. "Maybe you should see a doctor?"

"Nah, it's no big deal. Probably the gaskets are getting ready to blow. Getting old, that's all."

Laura poured half a can of Snap-E-Tom into a beer glass and the rest was beer. "Here you go, darlin'."

Sarge drained the glass. "Ah, feel better already." She poured the rest of the spicy tomato juice and beer into her empty glass and took a gulp. "I wonder why they call it that: hair of the dog?"

"You're all full of burning questions this morning, aren't you, sunshine? *Similia similibus curantur.*"

"Say what?"

"Latin. It means the stuff that messed you up will cure you."

"No doubt, a loose translation."

"A little loose, but you get the idea."

"Dog hair?"

"If a dog bites you, snip off a little of his hair." Laura talked with her hands as if she was snipping hair. "Make a poultice out of it," she made an imaginary poultice out of the hair and bandaged it on Sarge's arm, "and bandage it on the wound."

"Sounds like it would make things worse. You know how dirty dog hair is," Sarge said, brushing off the imaginary poultice. "What was that Latin saying again?"

"*Similia similibus curantur*. Don't knock it. It's the basis for homeopathic medicine. Vaccines. Check it out. A little dead virus of the thing that can kill you can keep you from getting sick."

"The Romans were good soldiers, but I think they were better at taking lives than they were at saving them. Hair of a dog, not buying it." Sarge nearly finished her drink with another gulp.

"You want another one?"

"No thanks. Got to stay straight for Christmas, got work to do. Going to get a J-O-B. You know, just for Christmas. Got any aspirins?"

Laura reached for a mega size bottle of store brand aspirins by the cash register and gave Sarge a couple. "I ought to get a nurse's uniform."

"You do that, and I'll marry you. Something about a nurse's uniform." Sarge washed down the aspirin with the rest of her drink. "Ancient TV saying: four out of five doctors recommend Bayer aspirin. But throw the doctors to the lions. What do they know, anyway?"

"Coffee?"

"Sure. Thanks. The world needs more of your kind, Laura. A little kindness goes a long way for greasing the sandpaper of life that's rubbing your ass raw."

"Look at you! Going all Ben Franklin on me with those wise sayings 'sandpaper of life.'"

Sarge started singing, "What the world needs now is love sweet love. Lord, we don't need another mountain. ..."

"Lord, we don't need another drill instructor caterwauling," Laura sung back.

"You got the want ads there?" Sarge asked.

"Want ads? There's nothing in the want ads anymore. Where have you been? Look on Craigslist, on your phone if you want to find something. Whatever you're looking for you'll find it there, plus some. Never realized there could be so many different combinations of relationships. Just like a Chinese menu, four ingredients get turned into one hundred dishes somehow."

Sarge took out her phone and found Craigslist. "Bingo, there it is."

Laura referring to her paper said, "They still haven't caught this guy. Can't believe it."

"What guy?" Sarge asked, looking down at her phone, scrolling through the ads.

"This guy who's been killing all these mini-mart clerks."

"What about him?"

"Some guy is going around the state, knocking off mini-mart clerks. He always takes a stack of girlie magazines with him. They call him the 'Hustler' killer. So far he's killed seven, and he's still out there." Laura showed Sarge a picture of the killer in the paper.

"Good enough picture of him. So what's the problem? How come they can't catch him?"

"He's on the move. Started out down south in Hollywood and has worked his way north - Bakersfield, Fresno, Stockton. A different victim in a different town. Apparently this is the first good picture they've had of him, probably getting over confident."

"Or wanting to get caught. It could be worse. He could be after bartenders."

"Do you think?"

"How many did you say he's killed?"

"Seven."

Sarge showed the phone's screen to Laura and said, "Here we go! Santa wanted!"

"What?"

"Santa. I'm going to get a job as Santa. What do ya' think?"

"I think it's a fantastic idea. You would make a great Santa."

"Really, or are you just saying that?"

"I think the kids would spend the rest of their lives in therapy after sitting on your lap."

"How can you say that?"

"Because you spent your life in the Marines, and it shows. Underneath, you're a teddy bear, but on the surface you're a grizzly. I think your smile is going to scare the kids. Besides..."

"Alright already, I get your point. Soften it up for the kids. What do you think I am, an idiot or something? I get it. Kids love me. The young ones do at any rate. You can have those teenagers, mean little..."

"You're right. If that's something you want to do, go ahead on. You want another beer?"

"Nah. If I want to get that job, Santa better not get smashed out of her mind."

"That's it. You go girl."

Sarge started singing cadence, "'Ain't no use in looking down, ain't no discharge on the ground.'" Laura tapped out the cadence beat on a beer bottle with her keys. "'If I die on the old drop zone, box me up and send me home.' Go ahead, get me another beer," Sarge said.

Later the same day, Sarge walked into the personnel office in Shapiro's department store. She was wearing a business suit, had gargled away the beer breath with Scope and had slicked down her hair with gel. Three other Santa candidates, all dressed in red with white beards and flowing white hair, sat in the office, waiting for their chance to impress the interviewer with their "ho, ho, ho."

The first would-be Santa greeted her with, "Merry Christmas! Merry Christmas!"

Sarge said, "Merry Christmas."

The second Santa whispered to the third Santa, "Not much spirit."

"I agree," said the third.

A spontaneous duel of Santa schticks got started by Santa number one who said, "Ho! Ho! Ho!"

Santa number two got into the contest with a louder, "Ho! Ho! Ho!"

Number three said, "Watch this." He got up from his seat on the couch, grabbed his belly, which wasn't a stuffed pillow, and thundered in baritone, "Ho! Ho! Ho!"

All the first one could say was, "Dagnabbit!"

"Enough already!" shouted the receptionist. "If you guys are going to get rowdy and act up, I'm going to have to ask all of you to leave. You got it?"

"I'm here for the Santa job," Sarge said to the receptionist.

"Here, take this application and clipboard. Be sure to fill out both sides and be very neat. Mr. Slocum, who will be interviewing you, is very particular about neatness. If he can't read what you've written, you don't stand a chance. Here's a pen. It's first come, first serve. You've got three Santas ahead of you, so it'll be about an hour and a half before he can see you," said the receptionist, handing Sarge the clipboard and pen.

"Thanks. I appreciate the advice," Sarge said, taking the clipboard and finding a seat.

The third Santa had his interview and was leaving the office. He said to Sarge and the receptionist as he walked out, "And to all a good night. Ho! Ho! Ho!"

"It's like this every year. I dream about them, the Santas. Actually I have nightmares about them. I think it would make a good horror movie. What do you think?" said the receptionist. "You can go in now,"she said, opening Mr. Slocum's office door.

"I guess they're harmless, but you could be right. *Santa's Payback is a Bitch,* call it that," Sarge chuckled, walking into Mr. Slocum's office.

"What was that about Santa's bitch?" asked Mr. Slocum, who had an uncanny resemblance to a store mannequin with the crew haircut, tie, white short sleeve shirt, and black framed glasses. He motioned with his upturned hand for Sarge to take a seat.

"Oh, I was just saying to the lady out front that a good title for a Christmas horror movie would be *Santa's Payback is a Bitch*. Just a little joke," replied Sarge, sitting down in a chair in front of Mr. Slocum's desk.

Mr. Slocum paper clipped a job app with his notes, fidgeted with a box of paperclips, and searched for the proper words to express his dismay that Sarge, a would-be Santa, had used the words "Santa" and "bitch" together. He finally said, "We don't use the word 'bitch' in the building and certainly not around Christmas time and certainly not with the name of Santa. Firstly, the store has a reputation to maintain. This is a department store, not an establishment for exotic dancers. Secondly, Christmas is a hallowed time of year. It's our busiest season. It's God's gift to the retail industry. Without it, where would we be? Up the proverbial creek without a paddle is where we would be, hitting the rocks in the middle of dreary winter when no one in their right mind would want to go out in the lousy weather and shop. Thirdly, it's Santa for crying out loud! The jolly fat man who sold more bottles of Coca Cola than any professional athlete or rockstar could ever do in their wildest dreams. For many, far too many, children growing up in godless homes, he is the closest thing to a god that they will come in contact with. Santa's name will never be taken in vain, at least not around here. Do I make myself clear?"

"Yes very, very clear. I appreciate clear orders. I appreciate clarity. It won't happen again, but I was just joking with the receptionist about the guys who had been in here."

"Those *guys* are your competition. We only have one vacancy. We only need one Santa and one on standby in case one should go down for some reason."

"Any reason for Santa going down? I would think it would be a pretty hazard free job, not like being a roofer or an infantryman, or something."

"Alcohol. It's the holidays. We can't have the slightest whiff of alcohol on Santa's breath. The kids, you know. Besides, the parents are right there. And the meds, some of the Santas, the best ones, are on some heavy psychotropic meds. These are the Santas who are Santa the year round. You may have noticed one or two in your time. It's the Fourth of July, over a hundred degrees, and there's some old guy with a white beard, dressed up in his red costume, wishing everyone a merry Christmas. That's your competition. Genius or madness, call it what you will, but if they're taking their meds, you can't find a better Santa, so believable. I even begin to think that there's a real Santa after being around one of the good ones for any length of time. Santa is the most competitive job we have in the store. Even with my job, there's not as much competition. Santa is just something the insane and the good hearted want to be."

"Maybe it's a god complex?" Sarge remarked.

Mr. Slocum didn't think it was funny, giving Sarge a stern look that said didn't you hear anything I was saying. He told Sarge, "Give me your job application. I need to review it." He said it in a tone of voice that said he had to go through the formality of looking at the job app but had already decided not to hire her. Sarge picked up on his tone and realized getting hired wasn't going to happen, unless the regular Santa was off his meds, and Sarge happened to be sober when the call came to fill the downed Santa's boots. She decided to play along as if she thought she had a chance of being hired. It seemed like the proper thing to do since it was a job interview. She thought the chance of getting hired was about like a snow ball's chance of not melting in hell but didn't want to bring up "snowballs" and "hell" in a sentence, learning her lesson about "Santa" and "bitch." Sarge handed him her job application with only one job listed for the past thirty-five years, the Marine Corps. She confidently smiled when she gave it to the personnel manager, proud of her lifelong service.

"I see you haven't worked for the past two years. Why is that?" Mr. Slocum asked.

"I retired from the Marine Corps after thirty-five years, and I took a break from work, just traveled around the states in my camper for a while."

"What did you do?"

"Just traveled, taking in the sights, seeing the national parks, that sort of thing." Sarge didn't mention that "sort of thing" meant visiting most of the bars called Dew-Drop-Inn.

"No. I mean in the service."

"Right. My last assignment was at boot camp. I was the First Sergeant of a training company. Came in the Corps at boot camp and went out at boot camp."

"Why did you quit?"

"I didn't quit; I retired. After thirty-five years, that was enough. Most personnel retire after twenty years, that's the minimum. Do twenty and that'll get you the money," Sarge said, rhyming the last part.

"Didn't like it, eh?" Mr. Slocum didn't have a pension to look forward to after thirty-five years with the company. All he had was his 401K, which wasn't growing the way the glossy brochure had claimed it would with the caveat that "past performance was no guarantee of future performance." He resented all government workers, including the military, who still had a pension and could afford to retire. He was bitter about the system not delivering on what it had promised. It had promised that hard work, saving, and investment would lead to a comfortable retirement – not so much. His nest egg amounted to a two egg cheese omelet which was enough on the plate to carry him up to noon, but then what was for lunch - social security? "Now you want to be Santa Claus. Why?" Mr. Slocum took off his horned rimmed glasses, putting on an even more sourpuss look.

"I thought it would be fun," said Sarge, stroking her goatee.

"Fun? You thought it would be fun? When you're playing Santa, the whole world is watching. Everyone has their eyes on this department store. Ever study drama? Never mind."

"Does being a woman disqualify me from getting the job? If so, just tell me, and I'll be on my way. I can take it. No big deal. Did you ever think of a Mrs. Santa Claus? I know you use elves with Santa."

Mr. Slocum had never interviewed a woman for Santa before. He didn't know what the law had to say about not hiring a woman for Santa based upon gender, but after being taken to court a couple times for discriminating illegally, he was shy about speaking his mind. He didn't want to say anything that he would have to later deny after getting legal advice. After going through the ordeal of being sued, he played it safe by ending every job interview with pointing to a government poster on the wall and paraphrasing what was written, "You see, it's against the law to discriminate against race, creed, gender, or whatever. ...

"I have your job application right here, and I see that you gave your current phone number. If we are going to hire you, we'll give you plenty of notice so that you can find a costume. But, be aware, this time of year Santa suits are in demand just like quality Santas, so they go fast. Any questions?"

"I understand. No, I don't have any questions," Sarge said, standing up to leave.

"Want a little free advice? It won't cost anything." Mr. Slocum actually smiled a little with the pressure of the formal interview over.

"What's that?" Sarge felt a little empathy for him who was showing a surprisingly human side. She had been where he was many times over the years, dealing with personnel. Even in the military, things had to be done according to the book, or else they could come back and bite you.

"Always ask a couple questions. Two questions shows that you have interest in the job, but three shows that you can be a pest," he said, holding out his hand for her to shake.

Sarge shook his hand and said, "Thank you for your time."

"Well, thank you for coming in. We will call you if we decide to hire you for the position."

"Any chance for a Mrs. Claus?" Sarge didn't want to play Mrs. Claus. It was Santa or nothing for her, but she wanted some feedback on what she thought was a pretty good idea.

"It's not in the budget." Mr. Slocum had learned this way of getting out of most requests when he was just starting out and used it countless times over his career. That one phrase "not in the budget" could kill dead in its tracks something that might require some work from him without having to argue about it.

After Sarge left, he noted on the job application that he had read the government notice about equal opportunity to her, put it in the file marked "reject," found a Handi Wipe, wiped his hands, and dropped the wipe in a trash can. He got on the phone and gave the job to George who swore that he was taking his meds.

After a couple more job interviews, Sarge drove back to the Broken Promise. She parked her truck, locked it up and walked into the bar, still wearing her business suit. Vicky and Terry sat at the far end of the bar, drinking and violating the California prohibition about smoking in a bar. Laura greeted Sarge with, "Hey Sarge, what's shakin'?"

"Hi sweetheart, how about a Pepsi, and I want to pay my tab. Today's payday, and the eagle is flyin'. How much?" Sarge said with the day's failure in her voice.

"Yeah, sure. Still on the wagon? You look good. A little bit of sobriety is a beauty secret I've been meaning to try one of these days, myself." Laura served Sarge a can of Pepsi and showed her the tab on a three by five card that read, "$247.89."

"Thanks," said Sarge and took out her wallet, putting the cash for the tab on the bar. "Keep the change. Shake you for the music?"

"Okay, but just one flop. I still have a headache from this morning's hangover, and all that banging I really don't need." Laura whispered in her cup of dice, "Come on little aces, time to show your little faces." She gently flopped them down on the bar.

Sarge shook her cup and told the dice, "Come on dice, do something nice for momma!"

Laura raised her cup. "A full boat, sixes over threes."

Sarge raised her cup and said, "Gotcha'! Four fives!"

"How do you figure?"

"Two fives and two aces," Sarge said, pointing to the two pair.

"I only see two pair. Where do you get four fives?"

"Aces are wild, right?"

"Did we say anything about aces being wild?"

"Well, we usually play aces wild."

"Only when we declare it before we roll, not after. Put some music in the box, Sarge."

"Might as well with the way things have been going today. So you want to hear some heavy metal or was that some rap?"

"Sarge!"

"Alright, alright. I'll play something soothing just for you."

"Thank you."

Sarge fed the hungry jukebox a couple dollars and had a hard time finding anything to bring up her spirits and bring down Laura's headache. She found her perch back on the barstool, hanging her saddlebag hips over the stool.

"So how's the job hunting going? I'm glad I'm not out there looking for a job. I hated that. Got to pretend that you're interested in what the dude is saying, smile and laugh at his jokes and all that. Hated it!"

"Nothing yet," Sarge said.

"Still looking for a J-O-B as Santa?"

"Yup, you got it."

"Anything else? Ever think of selling candy in Mrs. See's? Candy and Christmas - sounds like an easy enough sale. They probably let you eat all you want. That wouldn't be bad. I think they've discontinued the rum flavor, which is a real shame, one of my favorites."

"Just Santa, that's it. I don't need the money. It's not about the money. I just want to do it."

"Why this fixation with Santa Claus?"

"Because they tell me I can't."

"Who's telling you can't?"

Sarge turned on her barstool and faced the door to the outside world, the world of unwritten laws about who could do what and who couldn't. She waved her hand over the outside world and said, "Them! All of them!" then swiveled back, facing Laura.

"I hear that! So any leads?"

"I went out on three interviews and all of them said they would call me if they were interested. So the answer to your question is no. No, I don't have any leads. On this one interview, I could hear my job app hitting the bottom of the trash can before I got out of the office. Basically it's the same situation as it was thirty-five years ago. Some things never change."

"Before you left the office? Hate that when it happens. But, what did you expect?" Laura asked, wiping the bar with a bar towel.

"I don't know. With all the stuff you hear on the news and see on TV about human rights, women's lib and all that, I just thought things had loosened up a bit, that's all."

"Don't hold your breath. America has a very tight sphincter around its anus."

War's "Low Rider" played on the jukebox, "...low, low rider, drive a little slower. ..."

"All I know is that at these lousy interviews I get the same feeling that made me join the Marines back in the day. When I was a teenager, I don't know how many interviews I had been on and kept hearing "no." Then I walked into the recruiter's office, and it was different. They accepted me with open arms. Even on the first day, they took care of me and looked after me with three square meals and a place to sleep and people around to talk to. When I got to boot camp, there were a lot of women, like me, who had the same experience with the world. I didn't feel isolated anymore. It became more than a job or career; it was my home.

"I guess I can't blame them, though," Sarge said.

"What are you saying?" Laura asked.

"It's Christmas."

"So?"

"So it's their time of year to either make it or go in the red. They don't need some freak messing things up for them. They got to sell all that crap: the toys, the foot massagers, the night gowns, the perfume, all that crap. If they don't, they're in kimchi up to their necks," stated Sarge.

"Wait a second. Who's a freak? You aren't a freak. Don't you ever say that about yourself, girl. You hear me? We are the way the Almighty made us. If we are good enough for God, then we are certainly good enough for Mr. and Mrs. Buyer of Christmas Crap. Don't let me ever again hear you say you're a freak."

"You're right! I'm just feeling sorry for myself. I better give you twenty for all the whining." Sarge got down off the bar stool and started doing pushups. After one she was finished. "Well, you get the idea." She got back up, brushing off her hands, taking her seat back at the bar.

"How they see you is their own damn problem. If they can't see your beautiful uniqueness, then they've got the problem of being blind. If they are so small as to cast stones, then that's their damn problem not yours."

"It may be their problem, but their problem creates my problem of not getting a Santa's job, doesn't it?"

"If you were a man, do you think you would get hired as Santa?"

"Only if I was insane. I also found out that's another preference, at least Mr. Slocum's preference. You got to be a little crazy and trip on Christmas the whole year if you want a Santa gig at his store."

"Well you got the crazy part covered. Santa, jeez! While we're on the subject, this guy's birthday everyone is celebrating…"

"Jesus?"

"That's the guy. Look at where he was born, in a stable. That's some lousy marketing concept by today's standards. Not exactly the image that the shiny middle class likes to associate with, now is it? How's that going to sell perfume? Maybe a pitchfork."

"Missing your point."

"Images and reality, reality and images. Here this blue collar carpenter is preaching love for everyone, and the uptight hypocrites who claim to be his followers build walls instead of bridges. You see what I mean?"

"Yeah, I see. Don't be too hard on them. We all have our hang-ups. You and me and everyone. Like the bumper sticker says, 'Don't tolerate intolerance.'" You're an idealist, Laura. That's good; the world needs more idealists."

"Don't start singing again. So how are these interviews going?"

"I told you. Let's not go through that again," Sarge said, taking a drink of her Pepsi.

"No, I mean in your presentation. How are you coming across? If you go in there with all those negative vibes of expecting to be rejected, you'll get rejected."

"It's good. I'm sharp. Look at me. Not to worry, Sarge knows how to give a good interview."

"I used to work in personnel. I know how it works."

"Oh, yeah? For who?"

"Telephone company for twenty years, then I got this dream come true." She tapped on the bar. "What was I thinking?"

"So give me the skinny. How does it work?"

"If you want some advice, don't let on like it's life or death, or else you'll never get the job. It must have something to do with group behavior where the weak and injured get torn apart by the other chimpanzees. You want it enough to show the boss that he can lord it over you, but you are not going to die if you don't get it. You don't want to give those mean bastards out there the satisfaction of disappointing you. So don't send them a message that they'll be rewarded by rejecting you. You follow me?

"Whatever you do," Laura continued, "don't come across like someone with an attitude. The last person anyone wants is someone filing grievances and lawsuits. Eighty-percent of personnel's energy is spent on just one crusader. So don't come across as a Crusader Rabbit with a chip on his shoulder.

"I remember this one black dude who was going to fight racism wherever he found it. You talk about a pain in the ass! They finally got rid of him, but it took a lot of work. But in the end, he was gone. You hear me?"

"Thanks for the insight, Captain Obvious."

"You want the job or don't you?" Laura commented as if she was going to end the conversation and go back to reading the paper if Sarge wasn't going to take her seriously.

"Okay, I'll play the game. Don't worry about it, I come across good, servile but not too servile." Sarge stuck her nose in her fist as if she were brownnosing.

"Alright then, let's do a little roll playing. I'll be the personnel dude or dudess, and you be you. Let's give it a knock, knock."

Sarge knocked a couple times on the bar. Vicky and Terry turned their attention to Sarge, then turned their attention back to themselves.

"Come in."

"Hello Mr. Personnel Manager, my name is Sarge."

"I see that you were in the Marines. What did you do?"

"I did thirty plus, a lifer to the bone."

"No, I mean what was your job?"

"My last assignment was First Sergeant in a training company, boot camp."

"And what does a First Sergeant do in boot camp?"

"I turned daughters into Marines. When the company would fall out, I would tell them, 'When I holler attention, I want to hear a hundred and twenty mousetraps snapping shut at the same time. You got it?' and a hundred and twenty women would holler, 'Yes, First Sergeant!'"

Laura had to laugh. "And does Santa want the kiddies to holler yes, Santa? Or is Santa going to cut them some slack?"

"Santa is going to cut them some slack."

"Good! Good answer! By the way, where did you get that beautiful 'Spam' t-shirt?" Laura asked, pointing at Sarge's chest who was wearing a "Spam" t-shirt under her suit jacket.

"Watch it, Mr. Personnel Manager! Or I'll sue your ass for sexual harassment!"

"Well, I don't see why they wouldn't hire you on the spot. I think you've got it." Laura went into an act, mimicking *My Fair Lady*. 'I think she's got it. I think she's got it.'"

"All I know is that I'm going to be frickin' Santa Claus this Christmas one way or another," Sarge said with a determined look on her face, which matched her voice.

A couple days passed and Sarge went out on a couple more job interviews with their cold reception and unspoken rejection written all over the faces of the interviewers.

Sarge thought when the going gets tough, the tough get going. She started jogging. The physical punishment hardened her will to succeed in being Santa. Even when some troll in a passing car hollered, "Give it up, fatso," she jogged an extra mile. Memories of marching and double-timing in the Marines filled her mind, and she was homesick. She wondered why she ever left the Corps. She was so satisfied back in the day; civilian life sucked.

After one more discouraging interview, Sarge headed over to the Broken Promise. She hadn't been in the bar for a couple days, about the longest she's been absent from what had become her new home in her retired life. She walked in the bar, and Laura greeted her with, "Hello, *mon ami*. How's the world treating you?" To Sarge, the greeting sounded almost like mommy, mommy, you're home.

"The world's got its combat boot up my butt. Let me pay my tab, would you?"

"You paid a couple days ago. Don't you remember?"

"Oh, yeah. That's right. I forgot. Get me a Pepsi and get one for the rest of them in here and one for yourself, okay sweetie?" There was one customer sitting at the bar and a couple shooting pool.

The customer at the bar, took a drink of white wine paid for by Sarge, raised her glass and said, "Thanks, Sarge. Celebrating something? All dressed up and everything. What's with the Pepsi? Going to AA these days?"

"AA? Not really," replied Sarge, thankful that someone was taking some interest in her life.

The customer said to Sarge, "I used to do that when my daughter was alive. During the holidays, I would be sober for her sake. The only way I could do it was to go to AA meetings from the first of December to after New Years. Then I wouldn't see her for another year. I did that for thirteen years. Every year it was the same thing. I was sober for the month of December and two days in January. The rest of the year, well you know."

"She doesn't mind you drinking now?" Sarge asked.

"She died," the customer said without any emotion, as if she were numb.

"Sorry," Sarge sincerely apologized.

"Once she was gone, I lost my motivation. Now, Christmas, New Years, what's the difference, just another day."

"But, the AA thing worked for you?" Sarge asked.

"Yeah, it worked, but forget it. You know what I mean. That total sobriety ain't for me. I just as soon as have a couple beers now and then. If I get smashed once in a while, so what?"

The talk about AA was making Laura a little uncomfortable. Laura thought from time to time about her actions of aiding those with an addiction to alcohol, and she couldn't justify making a living off of those with what some called a disease. Laura changed the subject by asking Sarge, "Getting any calls about the job?"

"Yeah, I got one."

"See, I told you. It's attitude. Attitude equals altitude. How much are they going to pay?"

"Hold your horses. I had this message on my recorder when I got home…"

"And?"

"And I called them back, and they said it was a mistake. They got me confused with someone else. They got the telephone numbers mixed up, that's all."

"Crap! Don't let it get you down. They can't keep a good woman down, not for long that is."

"One problem."

"What's that?"

"I'm running out of time. Christmas doesn't wait for anyone. It's always here December twenty-fifth, no matter what. When the calendar says it's here, it's here."

"So you still aren't drinking anything? Totally sober?"

"Totally sober. Why, you think I'm an alcoholic or something?"

"I didn't say that." Laura hunted through her handbag for a mint. "Did I say that? Did I say that?"

"No, you didn't say that, but I know you. You're thinking it, aren't you? Go ahead and admit it. You're thinking I'm a drunk!"

"Are we a little touchy today, or what? How do you know what I'm thinking? I just think that it's really good that you are able to go cold turkey like that and stop drinking completely, especially the beer. I know you like your beer." Laura found a mint and popped it in her mouth, sucking on it.

"You're right about that. I grew up on beer. I think my dear mother had it in her breasts. Don't worry. You aren't going to lose a customer. Once Christmas is over and I've reached my goal, I'll be back enjoying myself."

"That's good. Accomplish your goal, then go back to enjoying life. You've been kind of grouchy lately. That's all. I'm not worried. I don't lose many of my customers to sobriety. Usually it's traffic accidents, or they just get too old to climb up on a barstool."

Sarge started laughing to herself.

"What's so funny?"

"That's a bizarre thought. Imagine it, a bunch of eighty year old gals sitting around, getting drunk, shooting pool, and trying to pick up on young chicks."

Sarge got off her barstool, left a dollar tip on the bar, and started walking towards the door.

"Where you going?" Laura asked.

"Got to get out of here before moss starts growing on my north side."

"Going to a church meeting?"

Sarge did a pretty good impersonation of the Church Lady, "Isn't that special."

Sarge got in her truck and headed north on Stockton Blvd., heading for her apartment in downtown Sacramento. She turned on the truck radio, and scanned for some Christmas carols. Every time a talk show came on, Sarge cursed it with "a'hole." Finally she found Bing Crosby singing "I'm dreaming of a white Christmas…"

She approached a red light and eyed an old watering hole of hers, a VFW bar. She thought she hadn't been in there for a while and should stop in to see how some of her old cronies were doing. She stayed away after a run-in with the bartender. She parked her truck and walked into the dark bar. The smell of beer triggered her compulsion. The first words out of her mouth were, "Give me a beer."

"What kind?" asked the bartender. It was the same bartender she had a history with. He had gotten abusive with a drunk customer, and Sarge jumped in, defending the drunk.

"What do you have on tap?"

"Pabst Blue Ribbon."

"That'll do. Give me a tall cold one."

The first one opened the weir to her compulsion to drink another. After the second, there wasn't a shred of free will to say "no" to another, then another. She spent the next four hours drinking beer, not saying a word to anyone, mostly thinking about the interviews she had recently been on. The anger in her fermented and bubbled. She fantasized about sending Mr. Slocum a package bomb or maybe burning down the store.

"Give me another one, would ya'?" Sarge slurred.

"Why don't I call you a cab, Sarge?" suggested the bartender.

"I didn't ask for a cab, damnit! I want another beer! Give me another beer!"

A couple other customers down at the end of the bar looked over at the spectacle the old sarge was putting on and wondered who would win the battle, the bartender or the drunk?

"That's it! Give me your car keys! You're too drunk to drive, and you sure as hell ain't getting another drink!"

"Come on, give me another beer. Just one more, and I'll leave. I swear," Sarge pleaded.

The bartender had won. He saw another alcoholic squirm for another drink, and he didn't give it to her. Now, he could really tear into her. "Get out before I call the cops! You're eighty-sixed. You hear me? Get out, you lousy drunk!" shouted the bartender, dangling Sarge's truck keys in front of her face.

Sarge lunged over the bar counter and snatched her keys. "Those are mine," she said and walked to the door. As she left the dark bar, the last thing she heard was the bartender telling the other customers so Sarge could hear, "Lousy, drunk dyke!"

Sarge got in her truck, thought about going to sleep in the camper but had enough of the VFW. She thought about crashing her truck through the front doors of the bar, but decided against it. She wanted to get away from the hurtful situation and back to her apartment where she could get some sleep and a shower to wash away the insults. She fired up the truck, turned on her head lights, and headed north on Stockton Blvd.

A city police car with its red and blue flashing lights and short blasts of the siren closed in on Sarge from behind. Sarge saw the police cruiser in her rearview mirror. She thought, oh crap! pulled over and put the truck in park. The cruiser passed her and stopped a car up ahead with a tail light that was out.

Sarge breathed a sigh of relief. She had never gotten a DUI, but her truck had a couple whiskey dents in the two front fenders. She had accidentally backed into plenty of parked cars in her time, but the heavy-duty back bumper showed no signs of her negligent drunk driving.

She sat there in her parked truck, turned off the ignition and watched the cop up ahead go through his drill of using the stop as an excuse to search the car, give the driver a field sobriety test, and check for outstanding warrants. Another cop car rolled up on the scene as a backup. They handcuffed the driver and put him in the back of the first cruiser.

The next thing Sarge knew, a passerby was banging on her window and shouting, "Wake up! Wake up!"

Sarge had fallen asleep, long enough for the truck's cab to grow cold. She nodded to the passerby, turned on the ignition, which barely cranked over the engine because the lights had been left on, and the battery was on its last charge. Getting a new battery was something Sarge had been meaning to do for a couple weeks. The engine barely turned over, a spark plug ignited the gas in one of the cylinders, the engine belched smoke out the exhaust pipe, and Sarge was on her way, still heading home.

She drove to her apartment on F Street, which was a Victorian house built in 1890 out of mostly redwood and converted into four one bedroom apartments back in the 1950's. Drivers had to have a permit to park on the street, which was only issued to residents. None of the converted Victorians had garages. Sarge was in luck because there was a vacant spot right by the cross street, making it easy for Sarge to just pull up and park, which Sarge did, but she still managed to bump into the back of the old Chevy station wagon parked up front. The bump woke up the man sleeping in the back.

No one knew the name of the man who slept in the back of the Chevy; even though, he had been living like that for over a year. People in the neighborhood said he was an ex-engineer for the State who had been fired for blowing the whistle, something about toxic dumping by one of the agencies. He was supposed to be fighting his termination in court, which was taking forever to grind out a verdict. In the meantime he hadn't cut his hair, shaved his beard, washed, or smiled. He ate his one meal a day down at Loaves and Fishes, a soup kitchen for the homeless and the poor. For some strange reason, no one complained to the city to have him and his Chevy towed away, which was remarkable, because if someone else tried to park on the street without a permit sticker on their windshield, he would get a ticket and his vehicle towed for a repeated faux pas. Some of the residents said the man in the Chevy was a saint living a holy life of self-denial. Sarge thought of him as being just another bitter old man who got hung up on getting even instead of getting on with life.

Sarge got out of her truck, not bothering to lock it. The man in the Chevy was sitting up, shouting at her, "Watch it! Damn you!"

Sarge shouted back, "Sorry!" She staggered up her walkway to her apartment on the ground floor, opened the front door, which wasn't locked, walked inside, turned on the light, and was greeted by her piebald black and white cat, General. Sarge bent over to pick up General, who was rubbing herself against Sarge's leg, but Sarge lost her balance and fell forward, knocking over a six foot Christmas tree. Sarge thought about getting up, but instead curled up in a fetal position on her side, stuck her thumb in her mouth, and fell asleep. General curled up beside her. The only noise was the cat purring and Sarge sucking her thumb.

While Sarge was passed out next to the fallen Christmas tree, two uniformed Sacramento City police officers, Randy and Bill, were in the mini-mart a block down from Sarge's place, getting coffee. After they got their coffee and paid for it, they walked out, nearly bumping into a skinny guy in a camo field jacket and camo beanie, who looked like the poster boy for the reason to say no to meth. The skinny druggie looked like the serial killer, "Hustler," because that's who he was. He was in a nervous hurry, high on meth, as he nearly bumped into the two cops who were walking out of the store through the swinging glass door, carrying their cups of coffee.

"Hey! Hey! Slow down, partner. You nearly spilled my coffee," said Randy.

The two cops walked over to Bill's cruiser, which was idling with the engine on, and got in with Bill behind the wheel.

"Does that guy, that druggie look familiar to you? I've seen him before," Bill said, drinking his coffee.

The two cops had been warned not to take their break in a public place, like Starbucks, because a citizen had videoed them taking an hour break and uploaded it to YouTube, causing embarrassment for their supervisor and the department.

"Let me think - medium height, skinny white druggie, wearing a beanie. Yeah, I've seen about a million that look like him," Randy said with a smirk.

"No. I mean I've seen him somewhere."

"Probably someone you've busted back when, and now he's all grown up and rehabilitated," Randy said sarcastically.

"Yeah, probably."

"You know, last night I almost shot someone," Bill said.

"You weren't working last night, were you?"

"Nah, I was at home. Heard this noise outside, about ten o'clock, out by the back fence. I got my gun and went out there to check it out. I shine my flashlight along the fence, and this kid's got his head stuck in my fence. All I see is his head sticking through the fence. I ask him what he's doing, prowling around, and he says that he's looking for his dog. He says can I help him get his head out. It's stuck; and he can't get out," Bill said, taking his time to tell his story, dragging it out to fill up some of the night with a little entertainment.

"So, did you?" asked Randy, taking a swig of coffee.

"You have to ask?"

"Well did you?" Randy asked with a big sardonic tone in his voice.

"You think I wouldn't help this dumb kid get his head out of the fence with it being freezing cold and all?" Bill asked.

"Well did you?"

"No!"

"I didn't think so. Meany." Randy got a cigarette out and lit it up.

"It'll teach him a lesson. Next time he sticks his head or his dick where it doesn't belong, he'll think twice." Bill swirled the coffee around in his cup, popped the lid to look at it, then put the lid back on.

"And he'll thank you, right?" Randy blew a cigarette ring, then tried to blow a smaller one through the first.

"I doubt it. Kids today don't know how to say 'thank you.' All they know is 'give me,'" Bill said, taking a drink of coffee, waving the cigarette smoke away from his face.

"I hear that. My sister's got three kids. Every time I go over there, which isn't a lot, I come away thinking I'm glad that I don't have any. I don't see why people have them. Just a big pain in the ass if you ask me."

"I know what you mean. You go into Starbucks and these yuppies bring in their brats like they're so proud of them. Like, look at me and see what I've got. The brats are screaming, running around, demanding this and demanding that. What a pain in the ass. It's enough to make you go out and get a vasectomy," Bill said, shaking his head in disgust for the whole family scene.

"Birth control – that's woman's work," Randy said.

"Got that right."

"It's a chemical thing."

"What is?"

"Being able to tolerate kids and think that you're enjoying it," Randy said, flicking his cigarette ashes out the window.

"You mean the parents are on Valium or something?" Bill asked.

"No. It's a natural thing. Hormones. When you're in your breeding years, you got your sex drive turned up with testosterone. It's one thing for nature to get you to screw your brains out, but now nature has got to make sure that you don't kill the annoying brats once you got them. So nature loads you up on chemicals that make you able to handle all that family life: the kids and wife with the nonstop nagging, and the never ending bills for stuff you thought you wanted but just turned into another annoyance, like cable or the boat sitting in the drive.

Check it out; once your breeding years are over, you turn into a grumpy old man. Nature got what she wanted out of you. You reproduced and didn't kill the kids. Your job is done. No need for loads of testosterone or the calming drugs. Nature turns off the spigot of feel good hormones and the least annoyance like a crying kid or a wife with 'this is what I want you to do today' sets you off. You've been used, dude. Mother Nature used you. The only remaining use for you now is to decompose into fertilizer. Get buried and fertilize the bushes and trees. Those natural drugs are some powerful stuff, man. Make you think you you're living the dream when in reality it's a big nightmare," Randy said, chucking his lit cigarette out the window onto the asphalt.

"What? You see this on the Nature Channel or something?"

"Nah. I was talking to Smokey about it. He was telling me ..."

"Smokey?" Bill asked in disbelief.

"Yeah, Smokey."

"Smokey? The pimp?"

"Yeah, Smokey the pimp."

"Funny you should bring up Smokey because I got an idea," Bill said.

"What's ya' got?"

"I got this cousin who works down in Hollywood."

"Hollyweird?"

"Yeah, Hollyweird. She's a producer or something on a new cop show. A reality show, you know. And she gave me a call to see if I wanted to be in an episode. You know, they would do a ride along. So I said 'yes' of course."

"Oh man. You know what this means?" Randy asked with a smile.

"Yeah, we're going to be on TV."

"This is opportunity knocking on the door. You hear it?" Randy cupped his hand to his ear and paused. "I hear it - knock, knock, knock. You hear it?"

"Not really."

"At any rate, this can bump us up on the food chain. It'll mean we can make detective next go round!" Randy said, letting his excitement show.

"How's that?" Bill asked, needing to be filled in on Randy's reasoning.

"Publicity! Free advertising. We get on the show and we give a good performance, talk it and walk it, totally professional like. When we go up before the board, they'll remember us. We'll stand out from the herd. Brand building. It's our ticket out of this uniform, man.

"I'm going to get some good suits. I heard about this tailor who'll make you a custom suit for just seven hundred in any fabric you want."

"How come so cheap?" Bill asked, drinking the last of his coffee.

"He takes your measurements, finds out what you want it made out of, and sends it off to Hong Kong. Has it for you in a couple weeks. Globalization, man," Randy said, crunching up his empty paper cup.

"So how does Smokey figure in all this?"

"We need a good bust. We don't need the drunk guy in his underwear and t-shirt beating on his ol' lady. We can do better than that. You know the public loves their colorful macs. They eat that stuff up, man!"

"Yeah, but when they do the ride along, what if Smokey isn't around? Then what?" Bill asked, wrinkling up his brow.

"We'll make sure he is. And when we roll up on him, we slip a little dope in his pocket and take him in. It'll be a good bust. Good TV," Randy said, tapping Bill on the shoulder.

"Sounds like a plan, but how are you going to make sure he's around? He could be back at his crib kickin' it."

"Let's go find Smokey, and I'll show you. Don't worry about it. I'll talk to him, and he'll go along with it like a pig to slaughter. You know he's a legend in his own mind. He'll jump at the chance to be on TV."

"Let's check out Bunny's. He's probably in there. Meet you down there. See if he'll go along. He's always good for a laugh," Bill said.

"Hey, Pancho!" Randy said.

"Hey, Cisco!" Bill replied. The Pancho-Cisco thing was something they always said after a coffee break, going back to patrol.

Randy got in his own cruiser, and both cars drove away to Bunny's.

"Hustler," who had been looking at girlie magazines, watched the two cruisers pull away from the parking lot and out into the street with little traffic. He put back the magazine on the rack and got a cup of coffee, loading it up with French vanilla and four packs of sugar. He put a lid on the Styrofoam cup and walked back to the magazines. He picked up the magazine he was looking at and walked to the cashier.

"Anything else?" asked the Sikh cashier.

"A pack of Camels and some matches."

"Hustler" paid for his purchase and walked out of the mini-mart.

Randy and Bill walked into Bunny's Bar, in downtown Sacramento. Bunny, the owner was behind the bar working as bartender. About forty years ago she used to be a Playboy bunny and made a living off her sex appeal for most of her life. When that gift began to wither on the vine as grapes will turn into raisins, she ploughed her life savings into buying a bar. She built up a regular clientele by pouring stiff drinks and hiring good looking waitresses who knew enough about the vanity of men to laugh at all the customers' jokes. When poker swept the country, she built a card room in the back, hiring only women dealers, doubling her profits. She acted like a protective mother to the girls who worked for her, giving advice about men was her specialty. She talked about her man from time to time, but he never came around. No one actually saw him.

"Bill, Randy, how they hangin'?" Bunny asked.

"On this freezing night they aren't hanging low, that's for sure," Bill told her, making like he was shuddering from the cold.

Bunny laughed at Bill's remark. He smiled back. "You want a little drink to warm you up?" Bunny asked, knowing they would say no.

"Can't. On duty. Somebody gets one whiff of booze, and it's all over. The job isn't what it was when my dad was walking a beat back in New York, for sure. Back then they treated you like you were a human being. A little shot now and then was no big deal. Now, they make a federal case out of it," Bill said.

Bunny fluttered her long black eyelashes and nodded her head as if she were being schooled.

"We're looking for Smokey. Have you seen him?" asked Randy who was eyeing the framed centerfold of Bunny, Miss March, taken back in the day.

"He was here a minute ago. Back there at that table. One of his girls is still there, so I guess he's around here somewhere, maybe in the gents or in the card room."

"Let's go check out the card room, partner," Bill said to Randy. They started to walk to the back room when Smokey came out of the men's room. Bill and Randy blocked the pimp's path, both assuming a dominating posture with hands on their gun belts, feet spread.

"Officers of the law, what a pleasure to see you on this festive evening during the time of our Savior's birth. Greetings and salutations to men of good will," Smokey said, enunciating every syllable of his flamboyant greeting.

"How would you like to be on TV?" Randy asked Smokey.

"I thought of a career in mass media on the small screen but chose a path in life coaching instead, but tell me more. Let's step over to my table where we can discuss what you came to discuss. I must admit, you have stimulated my curiosity." Smokey led the two officers over to his table, where he took a chair next to one of his working girls. His mink coat was on the back of another chair with his white hat. He was dressed in red and white, just like a skinny Santa.

"Feel free to speak in front of Channel. Channel will keep her mouth shut, won't you Channel?"

"Of course, daddy," Channel said. Channel wasn't anything to write home about when it came to her looks. Her main quality was her toughness in dealing with what happened to her on the streets. She had the delusion that Smokey would marry her one day, and they would have a happy home. This was her dream in life, but she didn't know how to get it. It was a mystery to her how other women were able to pull it off - husband, kids, and house - making it look easy.

"I know your woman can keep her mouth shut, but we need her out of here before we can tell you what it is that can take your career to the next level," Bill said, motioning with his head for her to leave.

Smokey didn't have to plead or even tell Channel to leave. All he did was look at her and raise his index finger, and she got her jacket, left the table, and walked out the door into the cold night. It was part of their image, an act upon the public stage. Randy and Bill admired Smokey for his ability to manage his women, or at least that's the way they perceived it. Bill and Randy did a lot of pleading in their relationships with women, having to expend a lot more energy than just raise a finger to get their way if they got their way. Despite being secret fans of Smokey's charisma, the two officers would never admit that they admired anything about Smokey. After all, the story was that Smokey was born and raised in a South Sacramento brothel.

"What do you want? How can I be of assistance?" Smokey asked the two officers.

"How would you like to be famous?" asked Randy.

"I am famous! All the ho's in North Sac, South Sac, all around the town know Smokey. I'm their number one life coach."

"I mean famous! Like famous across the whole nation."

"You mean across the land of the free and the home of the brave?'

"Absolutely."

"You mean where the buffalo roam and the antelope play?"

"That's right, right across the good old USA," Randy said, smiling.

"You mean in the land of where never is heard a discouraging word?" Smokey was smiling, showing off his gold teeth. Smokey was thinking, I'm the one who is really free. You aren't even free enough to have a gold tooth. You have to have porcelain, and you better not even think about painting your house purple. Conform, suckers. You're bound up by society's chains and don't even know it.

Both cops nodded yes, a little mesmerized by Smokey's rap.

"How can this be? Is a comet transiting Smokey's rising sign? What heavenly phenomena ushers in this fate for Smokey?" Smokey gazed out as if he were a ham Shakespearean actor on the stage.

"Television. Overnight you will be a celebrity, a star, a superstar. Have you ever seen *Cops*?" asked Randy.

"I see. And how, pray tell, do you plan to carry off this entertainment extravaganza on the tube?"

"I've got connections, Hollywood connections. The cameraman will do a ride along…"

"And lo and behold, you bust law abiding Smokey, making the two of you look good," Smokey said, running his trigger finger around the rim of his whiskey glass.

"No, we don't bust Smokey. We just pull Smokey over for a warning about his taillight being out. We get a chance to demonstrate our respect for your constitutional rights in a very courteous and professional manner, and you get a chance to show off your charisma with the way you do what you do. Get it? No bust, scouts honor."

"I guess that would make us a couple of show-offs then, wouldn't it?" Smokey looked Randy in the eye without blinking. Smokey had small eyes like a snake, which was a gift for surviving the street life. He never had to hit anyone. All he had to do was give a cold stare, and punks, thugs, and fools would back off.

Bill tried his hand at selling the idea. "It's about publicity, building a brand. You'll be building a brand! Without it, you just fade into the crowd of other nameless macs."

"I had a cousin once who was famous. It really didn't do him much good. Mail Fraud. He had his picture up in all the post offices all across the country. The notoriety really cramped his style, if you know what I mean," Smokey said, swirling the ice in his glass.

"Don't let this opportunity slip through your fingers. Grab it and make the most of it," Bill told him.

"Yeah, make the most of it," added Randy.

"I think this publicity could help my career as long as you let me star in this episode."

"Most definitely you'll be the star," said Bill.

"Definitely," added Randy.

"When is this going to take place?"

"We'll let you know when we get the details from the producer, probably in a couple months. Don't worry, you'll have plenty of time to prepare."

"I'm always prepared. You say it's *Cops*?"

"It's like Cops. You're in then?" Randy asked.

"I'm in like Flynn, Jim," Smokey said, flashing his gold teeth.

"Good decision! Good decision! You're going to be a star, man. We'll be in touch," said Randy, giving Smokey a soul handshake. Bill just nodded his head as the two cops walked out.

Channel walked back in the bar after the cops left and took her seat back at the table. "What's up with those two?" she asked Smokey.

"Those two? Just two crazy white boys who are up to something slick."

"Like what?"

"Why aren't you out working?"

"It's cold out there. I'm on my break. Besides, it's almost Christmas; cut me some slack. What's up with those two?"

"None of your business."

"I just want to know…"

"Why do you want to know for?" Smokey wondered why all the women he knew, none of them could shut up once they had the bit in their mouth but had to keep galloping ahead, paying no mind to the rider trying to get them to stop with the questions.

"I want to look out for you, daddy. That's all."

"You're confused, woman. I look out for you."

"So?" Channel asked, wanting to know the cops' business with Smokey.

"Damn, you just won't leave it alone, will you?"

"Just want to know, that's all."

"You don't need to know."

"But I want to know. No harm in just knowing, is there?"

"I said, you don't need to know."

"Come on, tell me. What did those two cops want?"

"Okay! Okay! If it will shut you up, those two turkeys want to set me up for a bust, probably plant some dope on me or something, so that they'll look good for some TV show."

"TV! I always wanted to be on TV."

"That's the last thing we need. When that thing comes down, Smokey and Channel are going to be kickin' it in Reno or somewhere."

"A vacation, daddy?"

"Sure, baby. A vacation, a working vacation." Smokey took a swig of his Chivas Regal and gave Channel a reassuring smile with his gold teeth.

Sarge sat on her regular barstool in the Broken Promise. "Two more days and it's Christmas. What are you going to be doing, Sarge?" asked Laura.

"You going to be open?" Sarge was drinking a Pepsi.

"No way. Not this Christmas. Going to Oakland to be with family, mom and dad. My sister with her kids should be there too."

"You looking forward to it?" Sarge asked.

"Yeah, of course. Should be fun."

"What's the hardest question you ever had to ask yourself?" Sarge asked.

"That's easy. Whether I was a lesbian or not. I really was confused about it. I guess that's why I got married. I really didn't know," Laura said, drinking a 7-Up.

"That's because you're feminine. You got confused because you're so feminine. It wasn't that way with me. Look at me. You think I got confused? No, I never got confused. I guess that's the silver lining in being butch - never get confused." Sarge took a swig of her Pepsi.

"So did you ever think of a sex change? You know, go all the way."

"Nope. I'm a woman and that's what I want to be. Like I said, I'm not confused."

"Sorry the Santa thing didn't work out for you, maybe next year."

"Who says it didn't work out?"

"You didn't get a job, did you?" Laura asked, knowing the answer.

"I said I was going to be Santa. Didn't say that I had to get a job to be Santa, did I? Speaking of which, I better shove off and buy some candy for the kids and get my costume ready, shine my boots and all that good stuff."

"Before you go, tell me what's been the hardest question for you, you know, about yourself?"

"If I could stop drinking. Do you think I'm an alcoholic?"

"They tell me that if you, yourself, can say that you are, then you're on your way to getting sober. I can't say if you are or not. You'll have to answer that one, but I can tell you that there aren't many I know who crash in their camper in my parking lot. You feel me?"

Sarge was back in her apartment, sitting in her La-Z-Boy velour covered recliner, spit polishing her combat boots, drinking beer, smoking cigarettes. She had an old t-shirt tightly wrapped around two fingers, applying Shinola and using the lid of the can for holding water. She applied a little wax, rubbing it into the leather, then dipped the rag into the water and used it to bring the wax to a high polish reflecting her image. This ritual, which she had practiced for thirty-five years, put her mind at ease. After her boots were polished, she set them aside by the chair.

She turned on the TV and watched the news, opening another can of beer. A six-pack of empties were on the coffee table. The local news broadcasted that "Hustler" had killed another mini-mart clerk last night in mid-town Sacramento. There were no witnesses, and the store's security camera was inoperative. The announcer speculated that the killer would continue traveling north after this homicide as he had done in the past.

Sarge continued watching TV, drinking beer, and smoking. She dozed off. A lit cigarette fell out of Sarge's hand during her snooze and fell between the chair's cushion and frame, setting the chair to smolder. The smoke alarm in the kitchen went off with its shrill noise, waking Sarge from her drunken sleep. Smoke was filling up the apartment.

Sarge got up with a jolt and shouted, "Damn!" She pulled the cushion off, which was giving off more smoke than fire. She poured the water from her goldfish bowl on the burned area, keeping the fish in the bowl by pouring the water through her spread fingers acting as a strainer. Her goldfish, Henrietta, was flopping on her side in the empty bowl. Sarge got more water for her fish out of the kitchen and filled up the bowl. She opened up a couple windows to air the place out. The alarm was still shrieking. She took it off the wall and buried it under her bed mattress, muffling the noise. Her cat, General, walked about, following her, wondering what was going on.

Sarge picked up General who had a scared look. "Well, kitty, did you think mommy was going to burn the place down? Come on, I'll make up for it and get you a treat, a nice can of Friskies."

Sarge walked with General in her arms, stroking the purring cat. She put the cat on the sink counter and opened up a can of cat food, emptied it into her bowl, and placed her cat and bowl on the kitchen floor. General ate her food with gusto because it was well past her normal feeding time.

Sarge noticed there was heat coming from the oven when she walked past it. She checked the gauges on the old white stove and saw that it was on at 350 degrees. She opened the oven door. The heat hit her face as she bent over to look inside. There was a chicken in there burnt to a black crisp still perfectly shaped, so perfect, Sarge could still see the bumps on the paper thin black carbon skin. Sarge turned off the stove and used a couple pot holders to pull out the Pyrex baking dish with the black chicken.

She put the Pyrex dish on the counter and stared at it. There was no smoke, no smell. She poked the breast with her finger, puncturing a hole. The chicken was hollow. All meat and bone had been vaporized. The black chicken was more of a shadow than substance. Remarkable, she thought. She remembered that she had put a chicken in the oven three days before. It had been in the oven at 350 degrees for three days instead of two hours. The thought of how lucky she was crossed her mind. The smoke alarm probably saved her from looking like the chicken - baked to a crisp. She thought she should be more careful in the future.

A banging on the door, snapped Sarge out of her introspection. "Coming! Coming!" she hollered.

Her neighbor, a woman student at Sac State, hollered on the other side of Sarge's front door. "You okay in there?"

Sarge unlocked the front door and opened it. "Hi. Yeah, I'm okay. No problem. Just burnt something on the stove, and it set off the alarm."

The neighbor looked over Sarge's shoulder and noticed the empty beer cans in the front room. "Sure, I know. It happens. Heard the alarm go off. You know this is an all wood building, got to be over a hundred years old, dry as a bone, and there's four apartments, so we all can go up in flames if there's a fire in one. What were you cooking, anyway?"

"Chicken."

"Sounds good."

"I would invite you in, but…"

"Hey, I would like to, but I'm on my way out."

"Christmas party, I suppose?"

"No. Going to an AA meeting. You want to come along, check it out?"

"Do I look like I need it?"

"I didn't mean to get all up in your business. I just thought if you weren't doing anything, you might like to come along. Something to do, that's all."

"Hey, that's really sweet of you. What's your name again?"

"Melissa."

"Yeah, that's sweet of you Melissa, but I'm kind of tired tonight. Maybe some other time."

There were only a few hours of shopping left on Christmas Eve, and the shoppers were out and about on the outdoor K Street Mall. Sarge walked around, wearing her Santa costume with a white beard and her spit polished combat boots. She saluted the shoppers with "Merry Christmas" and passed out candy to the kids. Some of the shoppers returned the greeting, but most were suspicious, not giving eye contact, thinking why isn't this Santa in a mall where he belongs. A young girl about six years old towed her divorced father, who had her for Christmas Eve, over to Sarge as if she were a sled dog tugging on her harness.

"Santa! It's Santa!" the girl hollered.

"Yes, it's Santa," the father played along.

Sarge crouched down to her level. "Have you been a good girl this year?"

The girl nodded her head up and down.

"What do you want Santa to get you for Christmas?"

"A puppy!" exclaimed the girl.

Sarge looked up at the father who told Sarge with his facial expression and moving his head back and forth to tell his daughter no.

"A puppy? Santa would like to get you a puppy, a very cute puppy, but not this Christmas. Maybe some other Christmas when you are big enough to take care of the puppy. You'll have to feed her and everything. You understand? What else can Santa get you?"

"I want a puppy!"

The father came to Santa's rescue. "When you're older, sweetie, Santa will get you a puppy when you're older. I promise. Tell Santa what else you want."

"I want a puppy!" The child was on the brink of throwing a tantrum.

"Sorry, honey. What else do you want?" Sarge asked, pleading with the kid to ask for something else.

"A puppy! I want a puppy!" The child started to cry, then sobbed.

"Here, here's a piece of candy for you." Sarge thought the candy would shut the kid up and calm her down.

The child took the candy and threw it in Sarge's face. Sarge stood up and said to the father, "Sorry."

"Come on!" said the father, dragging the child away who wouldn't move her feet.

The child got dragged away, down K Street mall with passersby staring at the kid, the father, and Sarge. Sarge felt like a fool, completely hollow inside. She took her pillow case candy sack, held it by the closed end and flung all the candy out of it in a big arc, like a Rainbird sprinkler, onto the promenade. She pulled off her beard and threw it in a trash can. She shouted, "Screw it!"

One of the shop owners had been watching Sarge and called the police, reporting that someone suspicious was dressed as Santa, passing out candy to children, and causing a disturbance. The police dispatcher assured the caller that a couple officers were on the way.

About a block away from where the curtain came down on Sarge's Santa performance, she was approached by "Hustler." "You got some spare change?" "Hustler" asked Sarge in a demanding tone.

"What? Do I look like Santa or something?" Sarge snapped.

"If you had a beard, yeah! Never seen no Santa with just a goatee."

Sarge took a good look at the panhandler and recognized "Hustler" from the newspaper picture. Cold fear ran through her body, and she thought better not make him go off. "Sorry, don't have any money with me. You know, no pockets in this suit."

"That's more like it, a little common courtesy never hurts. You came really close," the killer said, giving her a menacing look meant to scare her, which it did.

Sarge turned and walked on. The killer stood their glaring at her, then turned and walked away, heading for a Subway sandwich shop. Sarge walked around the corner of a building, lowered her Santa pants, and reached into her Levi's pocket for her cell phone. She watched the killer walk into the Subway. She thought this was perfect; he was trapped inside getting a sandwich. She called the police, waiting on the line with her Santa pants down around her ankles.

"There he is over there, by the corner," Bill told Randy, pointing at Sarge.

"Hey, buddy! What's up?" Randy asked Sarge.

"Glad to see you guys! I was just calling…"

"Don't you think you better pull your pants up? Put away your phone and pull up your pants," Randy demanded.

Sarge complied with the officer of the law, pulling up her pants. "I just saw the killer, the guy in the paper!"

"You got some ID?" asked Bill.

"Driver's license. I got a driver's license."

"Well?" Bill said impatiently, waiting for her to show it to him.

Sarge lowered her Santa pants again and got her wallet out of her back pocket. Bill took a look at the license and handed it back to her, motioning to her with both hands to pull up her pants, which she did.

"This is what we want you to do. You listening?" Randy said.

"I'm listening."

"We want you to go home and enjoy Christmas Eve there. We don't want you on the mall or anywhere near the mall. You understand? We see you here, we'll take you in. Got it?"

"Sure, I understand, but listen to me…"

"No! You listen to me! I want you to leave the mall, and leave it now! If you don't, you're going to get locked up. I don't think Santa wants to be locked up for Christmas, does he?"

"No. But…"

"Turn around." Bill was getting out his handcuffs.

"Okay! Okay! I'm going." Sarge walked away, got about ten yards, turned around, and hollered at the cops, "The killer in the paper, the guy who has been killing mini-mart clerks is in the Subway shop down the mall. You can catch him…"

"We aren't warning you anymore, buddy. You better get going unless you want to get locked up," warned Randy.

Sarge started walking backwards and hollered, "I'm going, but there's a killer in the Subway shop. Aren't you going to check it out? Check it out for crying out loud!"

"Best be getting along, Santa!"

Sarge walked a block and turned a corner out of the cops' sight. She got out her phone, called 911 and reported sighting the killer. Randy and Bill decided to take their break at Bunny's.

"Give me another beer, would ya', Laura?" Sarge asked.

"I'm going to be closing early tonight at midnight. I got to get up early tomorrow and drive to Oakland, so this is last call."

Patsy Cline was wailing the blues on the jukebox. Vicky and Terry were shooting pool.

"Okay, fair enough," Sarge assured Laura.

"Are you going to do it again next year? You going to make some kind of annual tradition out of it?" Laura asked, passing Sarge a bottle of Miller.

"What? Playing Santa?" Sarge asked, drinking her beer.

"Yeah, playing Santa. You enjoyed it, right?"

"Loved it! You should have seen those kids' faces."

"So you going to do it again next year?"

"I don't know. Got to rent a Santa suit and everything. You know what I mean?"

"I'm glad you did it, Sarge. Good for you."

"I'm feeling kind of tired. It's been a long day. I think I just might climb up in my camper and call it a night if you don't mind." Sarge got off her barstool.

"Well, Merry Christmas, Sarge. See you in a couple days."

"Sure. Merry Christmas." Sarge walked out of the Broken Promise and got into her camper. She lied there in her sleeping bag, thinking about the day, wondering if the cops caught the killer. She closed her eyes. She felt her stomach start to regurgitate the beer. Sarge felt her stomach acid work its way up into her throat.

Coffee Bums

I was sitting outside Starbucks, enjoying my coffee, half decaf, half blonde, extra nonfat, trying to think of a poem, something good. Nothing. The best I could come up with, although I only gave inspiration about 20 seconds, was a skinny haiku.

A tall blonde nonfat

table outside nothing more

cell phones chatter noise.

It wasn't much; but it started the day off on a creative bleep, see what else would come my way. With that thought, two young women baristas, clip boards in hand, walked up to the guy sitting at a table opposite me.

The manager-in-training said, "Hi, Jason. Mind if we ask you some questions about the service you received today?" She would do most of the talking. The other one was Chinese-American and a knockout: long raven hair loosely piled on top of her head, eyelashes way out there, and dressed all in black with a gossamer blouse.

"No. Go ahead," Jason said.

"What's ya' drinkin'?"

"Iced coffee."

"Pike?"

"No, blonde. Pike sucks."

"How is it? Okay?"

"Yeah, it's fine."

"Service okay?"

"Yeah, service was okay. It's always excellent here. You know this is my home Starbucks."

"Well, that's good. Got any comments, anything else?"

"Since you asked, my wife and I were in L.A., and we went to the Starbucks there, but they didn't have any water. You see, my wife was born without salivary glands, and she needs to drink a lot of water. When I asked for a glass of water to go, all they had was this metal decanter with some small Dixie Cups, like the kind you find at the dentist."

"We always give out water, even to the homeless guy who comes around. I don't know his name," said the manager-in-training.

"I know you do. I see him, don't know his name either, drinking a venti water all the time," Jason said.

Knockout said, "I give him water."

"Did you complain?"

"Called corporate headquarters," Jason responded.

"That's good."

"You know I'm a gold member. Sometimes I'm in here twice a day."

Gold member? What was this guy talking about? Have I been missing something? And he used venti. He speaks Starbucks.

"What about our furniture, our interior and all that? How's that?"

"Here it's fine, but the Westman store ... I've talked to Dave about them. Here, let me show you what I'm talking about." He starts showing them pictures of interiors of Starbucks stores on his phone. The women are a little rocked back on their heels. "Oh, yeah, I got pictures!" Jason goes through about a dozen photos, detailing the pros and cons of each interior. The Westman store, the nearest rival, got blasted. The young women were hiding their gloating.

Then Jason got on the subject of Starbucks stock. Jason knew everything about it: price history, current P/E ratio, you name it and he knew it. The manager-in-training knew how employees could buy and sell shares. Knockout didn't know anything, and I lost interest in her at this point.

"Some baristas in the early days became millionaires. Just not a millionaire but a multimillionaire," Jason said.

Jason saw that I was paying attention, and he didn't seem to mind that I was listening in. I thought, "I'll tell them this joke when they ask me for the survey: I like my coffee like I like my women, strong and cold. That'll get a laugh. Then I'll make up some water story. But, maybe Jason won't like that. I might be disrespecting him by one-upping his water story…" I continued to think up a story as the three of them moved away, over by the entrance doors. Manager-in-training gave me a look that said she was highly amused by what was going down, one for the books. Not a customer from hell, but one from who knows where, a Starbucks super customer. She didn't know that getting a cup of coffee could mean so much. She just thought that was corporate propaganda they tell you in company indoctrination as a new employee. Maybe they were right. They weren't in the coffee business. They were in the people business.

Jason wanted to show them what he was talking about, something about water stains on the windows from mineral deposits. They eventually came back, and I had come up with a water story. I was ready. I'll even show them my haiku. The young women thanked Jason for his time and went back in the store. I think they learned their lesson to never again ask a customer for their input. If they had a complaint, fine, but never for their input. Let sleeping dogs dream about chasing rabbits.

What the heck? I was all geared up ready to go. Ready to make them laugh, and they retreated to safety behind the counter. Jason, you must have ranted on for half an hour. You cut into my time. Now where am I going to use my repertoire? How about on you, Jason?

"You a Starbucks employee or something?" I asked.

"Nah, just a customer," Jason said.

I told him, "Never used to drink Starbucks until they got Blonde. Pike sucks."

Jason gave me a knowing nod of approval for both my discretion in coffee as well as my conversion to Starbucks. I sensed he was baptized as a Starbucks follower.

We talked about coffee. We talked about Pike, Blonde, decaf, what happens to them over time, the chemistry, how they're roasted and various independent coffee shops that have come and gone in the community.

"The way you know Starbucks, I know Pollo Loco. I can tell you all about all their stores all over the state," I remarked.

"Oh, yeah?" Jason said with a look on his face that I too was one of them. The coffee buzz had me hearing Jefferson Airplane singing "...I can tell from your coat, my friend, that you're from the other side...purple berries...wooden ships on the water..."

"Don't go in the one in Bakersfield. It smells like a dead chicken with wet feathers," I cautioned.

We talked for a while about Pollo Loco: its menu, store locations, its business history, its recent public offering and its future as an investment. Then I said to Jason, "I was going to tell them my Starbucks water story but thought it might be disrespecting you since yours was true and mine is just made up."

"Nah, that would be alright," he said.

"You want to hear it?"

"Sure."

I told him my story, "I was in this Starbucks talking to this old guy, just like I'm talking to you, when he says to me, 'I think I'm having a heart attack! Get me some water, got to take my nitrate!'

"I go to the counter and the girl tells me, 'It's against store policy to give out water.'

"I turn around, and the guy is laid out on the floor, clutching his chest. I go to him and explain the policy about free water. I ask, 'You want something else?'

"He says, 'Blonde.'

"I go back to the counter and the girl says, 'Sorry. All we got is Pike.'

"I turn around and holler to the guy because I don't want to lose my place in line, 'ALL THEY GOT IS PIKE!'

"He says something but his voice is weak and I can't hear him. 'What? Can't hear you,' I say.

"He gasps then shouts with his last dying breath, 'No Pike. PIKE SUCKS!'

"I ask the girl, 'How about a decaf?'

"She says, 'We can do a decaf, but it'll take a couple minutes. Got to do a pour over.'"

Electric Sheep Looking for Friendlier Pastures

I thumped the visor with my knuckles. "*Voila*," I said, lowering the visor on the driver's side of our Toyota Highlander. "Check it out, stays up. They wanted two-twenty to fix it. Two hundred for parts and twenty for labor. But I got it for one hundred, eighty for parts and twenty for labor."

"How did you do that?" asked Molly.

"When the guy was writing it up, he said the visor was so expensive because of the light that was inside by the mirror. I asked if they had a visor without a light. He said they did, and it was only eighty. So, I said, let's put that one in. I told him I would have to give a five minute explanation to you as to why we don't have a light, but for one hundred and twenty in savings, the five minute explanation was worth it."

"I've never used that light," replied Molly.

"How many years has it been broken, flopping down and annoying us?"

"At least five."

"I told the guy that these SUVs were designed for women, the deciders. Women make the decision as to what kind of vehicle the family is going to get. Women want mirrors and lights. Men want gun racks."

"At least it's fixed now." Molly leaned over and raised and lowered the visor a couple times, making a creaking sound like a rusty gate.

"Don't wear it out. We want this thing to last." In the relationship, I'm the penny pincher.

I was driving. We were on our way to Point Reyes for a couple days of vacation with Mother Nature. This was our go-to place for a few days to escape the valley's summer heat. We had been here several times over the years. The extraordinary natural beauty of the National Seashore was the main attraction.

We had hotel reservations at a hotel where we always stayed just outside Pt. Reyes Station, which is a small town on the Northern California coast in Marin County. Marin County has a high per capita income as well as a high divorce rate.

There's a song by Tom Jones that goes something like, ". . . they don't know what love is ... baby, you can leave your hat on . . ." Everyone tries to define what love is. I say it's a mystery, and like a mystery it is beyond definition. If I were to write a love song, it would go something like this . . . they don't know what love is ... baby, you can leave your prosthesis on . . .

Sitting there, waiting for the traffic light to change, thinking about the commitment of marriage, my thoughts were interrupted by Molly when she asked, "What are you thinking about?"

I said, "They ought to teach marriage and family in high school. Teach them what it's really like."

Molly said, "Give it to them before they start dating."

"Yeah, before they get pregnant. They need to know what marriage is really like. Like when you get married, the sex stops."

Molly chuckled, "Right. Make the boys spend some time around some nuns and tell them that's how it's going to be. Then tell the girls the guy she's in love with will have his prostate removed one day, and he'll be peeing on himself and smell like a wet diaper all the time."

I said, "Make them go down to the Greyhound bus depot and hang out with the homeless dudes for a weekend. Tell them that their hubbies are going to smell like that one day." I mimicked an old woman school teacher, "Now girls, that's your assignment for the weekend, and I want a two page report on your impressions by Monday." I was on a roll. "Make the boys go down to Stockton, down to the Chinese shop that kills and cleans chickens and ducks. Tell them that their girl friend is going to look like one of those chickens, someday, on the assembly line, dangling there without any feathers on, white bumpy skin." We were having fun.

My eyes began to water with laughter, or was it the allergies? Molly was laughing so hard, she couldn't speak. We barreled down the road to our getaway, but first we needed a pit stop at a cheese factory, not the chain restaurant, but a creamery where they made cheese. We went there a few years ago when we saw their sign that read, "FREE GUIDED TOURS." Of course, there weren't any, just tourist bait. That time, and since then, we've gotten our pay back by scarfing down on the free samples of brie and crackers. It must be my Celtic blood to make me do such treacherous, vengeful deeds.

We pulled into their parking lot by the "FREE GUIDED TOURS" sign. The front door had a handwritten sign, the one it had for years, "NO TOURS TODAY." The two girls running the joint were new faces. They always were new faces, which helped, because they didn't know our modus operandi. We looked like bona fide buyers, sampling, standing back silently deliberating, all subtle body language of a buyer from the ranks of the consumer middle class. Then, after our fill, we were out the door and down the road. We were Bonnie and Clyde, but no one would get shot. It was just a piece of cheese.

When we got to Pt. Reyes, we had some time to kill before checking in at the hotel. Not much point in walking through the main drag in town, mostly boring little shops. Pt. Reyes makes its living off the tourists. The locals don't like the tourists, but they need them or at least their money. They have little shops that sell baubles and bangles made in China. You have to watch your step; the shop keepers are craftier than pirates.

I talked Molly into going horseback riding, "Ah, come on. It'll be fun." She had never been before.

My horse was a big old Belgium plough horse named Delilah. A wrangler would lead us around the trails through the woods and along small creeks for an hour. Paradise.

I told the wrangler, "No need to trot, walking is fine." Off we went.

Molly didn't get it, that the reins were there to guide the horse. She thought she should tell the horse where and how to go. The horse must have thought that he had a lunatic on his back who wouldn't shut up.

I refused to kick Delilah in her sides. I thought going for a walk without a jerk on her back would be a welcomed relief. Even a big old horse like Delilah must get fed up with people kicking her in the ribs. Think about it. So she meandered from one sweet spot to another, chomping on grass. After Delilah had a mouthful, she and Molly's horse would get behind the wrangler's horse and tag along.

About a half hour into the ride, two women riders in English riding clothes on Arabian horses came down the trail from the opposite direction. The hooves click-clacking. One said to the other, snickering, "Look at this horse," meaning Delilah. Her riding companion laughed. The first one again piped up sarcastically, "Where'd you get that roly-poly?" More laughing as they trotted down the trail. I looked back over my shoulder at the snob brigade bouncing along. Delilah farted a "goodbye." The wrangler didn't look back but appeared to take it in her stride as if the snooty behavior from the 50-something brats was an everyday occurrence.

We straggled back to the stables. Molly vowed never to go horseback riding again. "My horse wouldn't do anything that I told him to do!"

Her horse, Romeo, was probably thinking that he could take getting kicked in the ribs better than the micromanagement ordeal he just suffered.

Back at the hotel, I was lying on the bed looking at a brochure from the hotel lobby of things to do in the area. Sky diving, bungee jumping, and surfing weren't on our agenda. The brochure spoke of the Marin/Sonoma Coast Cheese Trail. Stalking free cheese samples were right up our alley. The brochure touted "artisan" cheeses. "Artisan" meant only one thing to me: they were going to give a little song and dance about how they were made from local this and local that, then way overcharge.

Tomorrow we would hit the Cheese Trail, but first I wanted to go to the beach. I wanted to get some photos because I was going through my seascape painting phase.

The next day I was on the beach with my little point and shoot. Molly was in the car. She didn't want to get the sticky sand in her shoes and on her feet. I told her I would be right back.

The beach was spectacular: blue sky and ocean, sandy beach, and green hills. The only thing wrong with it was the people. It wasn't Coney Island crowded, but the people on the beach spoiled it. I was taking photos up and down the beach trying to catch just the right moment of the surf's action. I felt someone watching me in a creepy way. A couple kids were splashing in the surf a few hundred yards down the beach. They were the only ones in the cold Northern California water.

I left the beach. I had only been there a few minutes. I stopped to rest on the other side of the dunes on a wooden bench to catch my breath after trudging through the soft sand. The bright warm sun felt good on my face. All was right with the universe. Then I heard her.

"Sir! Sir!" This woman was double timing over the dunes, waving her bony hands and skinny arms.

I thought I might have somehow dropped my car keys or something, and she was catching up with me to give them back. I stood up to talk to her. But before I could say anything, she went into her rant. Her voice started off low, non-threating, almost apologetically. "My daughter is upset. She says you were taking pictures of her."

Before answering, I thought, "What the heck?" I told her in a low calm voice, "I wasn't taking pictures of her or anybody. I was taking pictures of the beach."

She had sized me up and knew she could be as rude as she wanted, and I wouldn't yell at her or tell her she was crazy or punch her in the face. She went for it. She shouted, "I saw you! You were taking pictures. I want you to erase them. She's scared. You scared her!"

I got her drift. She was inferring that I was going to use pictures of her daughter for some creepy purpose. Not much point in defending my honor with indignation. She was a nut. I didn't want to get in a big argument with her about me having the right to take a few lousy photos if I wanted. I decided to just defuse the situation. "No problem," I said. "I'll erase them, ok?"

The air went out of her. In her mind, she had won. She calmed down. "All right," she said and walked away. But she couldn't leave it alone. As she was walking away, she turned around, walked backwards and said, "You're lucky I didn't call the police. It's against the law, you know." She kept walking backwards, waiting for me to say something. I didn't say anything. She turned around and walked over the dunes.

I got back to the car and Molly asked, "What's the matter?"

"I was molested by a woman, psychologically molested by a damn pedophile accuser." I told her how I had been violated by being, in so many words, accused of being a pedophile.

"Didn't you tell her that you're an artist? That you were only taking photos for painting?"

"Oh sure, artist ... little girl ... photos ..."

"I see what you mean, not a good idea."

"I didn't think she was worthy of an explanation. What kind of a person would say something like what she said to me? Wait a minute ... Do you think she's done that sort of thing before?"

"Could be. Takes all kinds. Forget about it, honey. Lucky she didn't run up and down the beach screaming PEDOPHILE!" Molly made the face of a screaming nut case, screaming, "PEDOPHILE! PEDOPHILE!" She had both of us laughing.

A couple birdwatchers, just back from their trek on the dunes, turned their binoculars on us and scoped us out.

I told Molly, "Okay, okay, people are staring at us."

Our second stop was a creamery in Pt. Reyes. We were on the trail. We were there for the cheese. The counter girl didn't look like she belonged in Pt. Reyes. She was young and attractive with pink hair. The local women aren't known for their good lucks or charm, but mostly for their trust funds.

As I said, Point Reyes is filled with cagey little shop owners. This cheese shop was shrewd all right. No cheeses left out for slicing into samples by free loading tourists. When we asked if they had any sheep cheese, the counter girl with pink hair whipped out a cheese and sliced off a couple micro thin samples.

"Try this," she said.

We did. She knew that it was going to take more work, more than a lousy one time sample to get me to go for my wallet. She kept working it, kept up the patter in a soft voice, so pleasant after the screeching scarecrow on the beach. All the cheeses –sheep, goat, cow - were great, never had better. I tried not to be seduced.

Molly was looking at the price on a hunk of cheese. She said, "It's only $9 a pound. Only a dollar more than I pay at the store."

The girl corrected her but ever so politely, "It's $39."

Molly thought the 3 was a dollar sign. That's right, I forgot – artisan. I felt the blood rush to my cheeks – fight or flight. Just turn and walk away. No, I'm such a coward. I'm afraid of being judged too cheap by this petite girl, afraid of a little girl with pink hair. Worse than a sissy. See if I can squirm my way out of this.

Molly to the rescue, "How long can this go without refrigeration? We're staying at a hotel and don't have a refrigerator. We'll be leaving tomorrow."

The girl parried and countered, "We've got these little waterproof bags and ice packs for a dollar. That'll keep it cool until you get home."

The girl with pink hair had us. I got my wallet out and bought a quarter pound of sheep cheese. I ate more than that for free at the cheese factory the day before. I guess it was sheep cheese. I was a little stunned by being outfoxed by the girl with pink hair. Molly got a little brie. Don't ask me how much it cost. I just forked over a couple bills and got some change. I was in a daze.

That night, back at the hotel, I was reading Philip Dick's novel *Do Androids Dream of Electric Sheep?* Dick had lived in Pt. Reyes for a while. I could see why he was attracted to the area with its natural beauty and, on the surface, its small town charm, but he didn't hang around long. He packed up his typewriter and followed his flock of electric sheep in search of friendlier pastures.

About the Author

Robert Hobkirk lives with his lovely wife, Jeannine, in Northern California. Besides family and friends, he enjoys nature, the arts, baseball on the radio, and ice cold watermelon on a hot summer day. He looks for art in the ordinary, which is taken for granted and in plain sight.

Robert has developed the short story "A Sure Thing" from *Blind Date* into a novel, *Tommy's Exodus*, and will publish it early in 2016.

Robert posts a blog at http://hobkirkartblog.blogspot.com/.

Made in the USA
Charleston, SC
23 September 2015